W9-AUX-153

Memoirs of
a Dog

by

CousCous Mackey

Artistic Origins
Bellaire, Texas
2002

Copyright © 2002 by Artistic Origins
All rights reserved. Published by:
Artistic Origins
P.O. Box 584, Bellaire, Texas 77402
877-611-8612 Toll Free
713-271-6812
info@artistic-origins.com

http://www.couscousbiz.com

Illustration & Cover Design by Michael A. Mayor
Edited by M. A. S. Stautberg

Mackey, Barbara D.
   Memories of a dog / by CousCous Mackey [as told to Barbara D. Mackey] ; illustrated by Michael A.Mayor ; edited by M.A.S. Stautberg. -- 1st ed.
   p.cm.
   Summary: CousCous tells her story of uncaring humans ; her mother, Feathers, and her dream of a happy life. Join CousCous in her touching journey from fear to loneliness to longing as she struggles to hold on to the only legacy left from her mother--hope.
   Audience: Grades 4-12.
   ISBN# 0-9701137-5-7
   1. CousCous Mackey (Dog)--Juvenile fiction. 2. Dogs--Juvenile Fiction. 3. Family--Juvenile Fiction. 4. Hope--Juvenile fiction. [1. CousCous Mackey (Dog)--Fiction. 2. Dogs--Fiction. 3. Familiy--Fiction. 4. Hope--Fiction]
I. Mayor, Michael A. II. Title.
PZ7.M1986345Me2002   [Fic]
                       WBI98-500037

The paper used in this publication meets the requirements of the American National Standard for Permanence of Paper for Printed Library Materials Z39.48-1984.

Printed in the United States of America

This book is dedicated

to the memory of Leo McBurnett,

who was killed in an incident of road-rage.

As well as to the millions of other animals

who have suffered

so dearly and needlessly

at the hands of some humans.

Table of Contents

Table of Contents *(Continued)*

Memoirs of
a Dog

Part I

Ill blows the wind that profits nobody.

—Shakespeare
Henry VI, III, II, 5.

CHAPTER 1

Hopeful Texas Mornings

Tedious. That's the word Mom used to describe a Texas summer to me, and over the years I have surely understood what she meant.

When the weather makes a change, it's a predictable one. Around the Galveston Gulf Coast and even as far inland as Houston, you have your choice of hotter or damper, and usually both. There are rainstorms, of course, and fierce ones, too. But you'd swear the showers they produce came spewing out of a boiling caldron. No sooner than the raindrops hit the pavement, the sun-baked cement vaporizes them into a steamy mist.

Those of us in dogdom know a little secret, though. We'd be happy to share our knowledge with humans, but humans don't always want to listen (especially not to a dog). Plus, humans never seem to have time. Which, of course, you *must have* to learn new things.

This particular secret has to do with the weather. Or more specifically, how a dog knows when the weather is going to change. Not a predictable, tedious change that even a cat can see coming. A big change. A magical change. A true blue norther kind of change. That's what we call them here. A wind so quick and cold that it sends the flimsy-furred squirrels running into the shrubbery to seek cover among the bushes.

In late August or early September, when the dog days have gone on for what feels like an eternity, a very special thing can happen. You must be patient, and you've got to be quiet, but if you take the time to notice, something quite out of the ordinary, something really quite *extraordinary*, can happen.

A deep north wind, quick as a cricket, sails through the sky. It runs down the tree trunks and blankets the old wooden barns, causing their planked sides to curl up and crackle. You're fooled at first. You think it's going to be just another cool snap *(those actually happen all the time)*, but it's not. *Not a true blue norther.*

This wind is a once in a lifetime event for most dogs, and when it comes it sends an icy chill down their spines. It arrives very quickly and never lasts for more than a owl's blink, which is why they have to be patient, but it gives them exclusive rights to the first breath of fall and the promise (or maybe the curse) of a long, hard winter. That's what a true blue norther is. Not a common occurrence in Texas, but one well worth waiting for.

Now, I'm not saying *all* humans would be able to experience an early magical norther like we dogs do. For most humans, their first knowledge of fall or winter comes much later in the season, closer to late September or early October. But, with out heightened sense of hearing and smell, and our natural intuition, and most importantly, our eager desire to commune with nature (the same abilities humans once had, too) we know a lot of things humans have forgotten.

Like most dogs, Mom (a purebred Pekinese named Feathers, by the way) wished for that magical wind but never really expected that it would ever come. Even without a blue norther though, Mom loved mornings best. Hoping for that jasmine scented rush was just one more way of passing her time, and keeping up her hope.

But on that late August day a true blue norther did indeed come through. For Mom, the timing could not have been better. You see, dog lore also has it that a true blue norther is a sign of new things to come. An omen of change. Naturally, Mom hoped the change would be for the better. But that was part of the mystery and the thrill. One never knew. One could only hope.

CHAPTER 2

The Winds of Change

The morning seemed no different to Mom when her *Humans*, the Granites, hurriedly rushed her out of the back door. It was 6 a.m. sharp and they were getting ready for work and had no time to dally.

Mom's outside frolic was the highlight of her day. She rolled and tumbled in the grass and bushes and played for as long as she could, always praying *The Humans* were not running late, which could cut her outdoor time quite short.

She ran after the squirrels and birds and turned over on her back to wiggle in the dried-out flowerbeds. She dug for phantom bones and chased shadows hiding behind the trees.

Whenever she could, she listened for the bark of Mr. Beaux, the dog next door. Although she'd never *formally* met him, his strong, firm barks and howls more than hinted at his strength and courage, and they reassured her. When he barked he knew exactly what he was barking about. He never yapped, and he only howled when the moon was full. Mom loved to listen to him howl. It made her heart stir. Her long-ago glimpse of him reminded her of how handsome he was.

I never got tired of hearing about the first time she saw him. It was several summers before this fateful blue norther day, and Mom was lucky enough to have had a few extra minutes out back. There was a loose board in the fence separating her yard from his, and Mom was very curious. She approached the wooden barrier excitedly, yet with apprehension. There was just enough room for her to get her nose and one paw into the space. She dug quietly and gently. After a few moments she could see into the adjacent yard. Mr. Beaux's yard. Her heart sank.

He was just barely in sight, quietly napping in the ground cover surrounding a large water oak. Mom could get a good view of the area, though. Humans say dogs are color blind, and it's true we don't see exactly the way people do, but animals have a way of knowing when things are pleasant and comforting. All the beautiful blooms with their different shapes and fragrances filled Mom's senses. The flowers were fresh and healthy, and there were a whole variety of blossoms and petals.

Across from the big water oak tree a large dark cushion, clean and fluffy, was placed in the shade. Mom could just make out the name "Mr. Beaux." A heart was embroidered next to it. A bowl sat beneath a slowly dripping water spigot that allowed a small trickle of fresh cool water to keep it full and clean, all day long. Bits and pieces of partially chewed rawhide bones and toys were scattered around, creating the feel of a huge play area.

"Oh, my," she thought. "He must be deeply loved."

Looking at him peacefully laying there in the morning sun, she had no doubt it was true.

Mr. Beaux was not a huge dog, like a noble Great Dane, nor as stern as a German Shepherd. His coat was not short, like a Doberman's, nor as long as a Retriever's. Certainly he had some Collie in his background (Mom could tell that because he looked so smart). And, Lab, too (Mom said she sensed a Lab because Mr. Beaux looked extremely reliable). But, her glimpse of him was so brief, sometimes she wondered how much she saw, and how much she imagined.

Tears glistened in Mom's eyes, and her heart was heavy and worn as she gingerly refilled the small hole, using her delicate nose to push the loosened board back into place. Once again, she surveyed *her* yard.

Years back it was neat and clean, and even cheerful, in a mundane sort of way. But things had changed. *The Humans* had stopped all the seasonal planting until dried weeds popped up here and there, harum-scarum, in the parched flowerbeds. Her yard had become shabby looking, with broken clay pots, and old cardboard boxes piled up against the garage. She reflected on how void of any character and warmth her world had become, and she felt an unbearable sense of loneliness.

That memory, so long ago, seemed particularly vivid and significant for Mom on this day. For somehow, even before the norther actually breezed through, Mom's intuition told her something quite different was stirring in the air.

She turned and scratched and sniffed, and finally settled down facing south—directly into the path of the oncoming wind. The first movement in the air gently rustled the soft hair framing her face, and her nostrils quivered as she took in the scent. Suddenly, very suddenly, complete stillness. Silence. Almost imperceptibly, her feather-like tail began to rustle. The wind had made an abrupt switch; it was now coming from the north. Turning her body to face it she stretched her paws and lowered her head and neck, raising her back and tail in a graceful arch. Like a supplicant, her head bowed into the oncoming wind, she submitted her will to the forces of nature.

Blades of grass and dirt particles whirled around her body, the sides of the sagging garage cracked and popped, squirrels left their branches on the nearby trees, scurrying into the bushes for cover, dark layered clouds whisked across the sky.

The true blue norther lasted just a short time, but its impact would be life-long for Mom.

Humans are very smart, some smarter than others. No dog would argue that. And so it is with dogs as well, some are smarter than others. As it happens, my Mom is one of the smartest.

The norther left Mom's yard as quickly as it had come, and as it crept through the neighborhood, the response from the other cats and dogs, spiders and squirrels, mice and mosquitoes was the same. Magic was in the air. The question was, would it be black magic or white magic? Or maybe a bit of both?

"GOURUFF, GOURUFF," she exclaimed.

Now this word, shortened by humans to gruff, gruff (and in some cases guff, guff) has more than one meaning. Out of context, it can just be a call to pay attention, sort of like, "listen up." Tone can make a difference, and body movement, as well.

In this case Mom's tone was unmistakable. GOURUFF. GOURUFF. This was much more than listen up.

"GOURUFF, GOURUFF! THE MAGICAL WIND HAS COME. CHANGES ARE IN THE AIR. BEWARE, BE ON GUARD."

By now, Mom's body was rigid and straight.

So mesmerized was she, it wasn't until Mrs. Granite's pointed shoe poked her in the side that Mom scurried back into the house.

CHAPTER 3

The Cold Stone Granites

It is the luck of the draw. Animals can be treated like anything from family members, to loving pets, to virtual prisoners. Unlike humans, they have no choices.

In Mom's case, her jailers were named Mr. and Mrs. Granite. Like far too many humans, they didn't buy Mom because they loved her, or because they loved dogs, or even pets in general. They bought Mom because it was "the thing to do" (plus, Mrs. Granite knew it would annoy Mr. Granite). Pekinese, like my Mom, were fashionable a few years back and Mrs. Granite, being the maven that she is, just had to have one. Pekinese, I mean, not Mom.

The Humans didn't beat or starve Mom, not right off the bat (that would come later). She might miss a meal or two, or her water bowl might dry up from time to time, but for the most part she was fed and not bothered with.

In fact, as time went on, she was *never* bothered with. Mom was a prisoner in solitary confinement. No longer considered a designer dog, she was relegated to the laundry room, like an out-of-fashion blouse. There were no more evening walks. No roaming around the house. She couldn't remember what carpeting felt like.

With the exception of Mom's morning tryst in the yard, she was locked away for days and weeks and now even months at a time. She served out her life sentence next to a mismatched rusted-out washer and clackity-clack dryer, never giving up hope that a change might come.

Dogs are pack animals who love to socialize, so living in such solitude was a hard adjustment, but over the years Mom learned to entertain and busy herself, and to make the most of her drab life. And the recent arrival of the mice in her life (Needles, Willie, and Bean) were her saving grace.

The Humans' constant placement of poisons and traps aimed at thwarting almost any living thing from entering the house caused a great obstacle for her new friends, but when they were able to navigate the terrain their visits were priceless.

Other times, Mom tried to keep to her routine. Each morning, after she had been secured in her cell, she'd start her day with viewings of the birds and squirrels (and anything else) she could see from the laundry room window.

She'd climb on the scattered boxes, up to the worktable. Dragging one of the tattered, musty blankets that served as her bed (unlike the pillow in Mr. Beaux's next door yard, this one had no heart on it) she would watch the activity through the small glass opening in the wall.

CousCous Mackey

When fall came and the trees lost their leaves it was quite easy to see the squirrels chasing each other throughout the branches. Mom would hold her breath when one fell off a limb, only to deftly grab a lower limb, and start the chase again. The blue jays, dive-bombing into the squirrels, attempted to create even greater perils for them on their treks.

The cardinals, never interfering, sat stoically on the power lines, draped in their silky red-feathered suits. Then, when they floated off into the sky, Mom would pretend she was flying with them. She would imagine herself sailing out of the laundry room window, soaring on the open air. Sometimes she would slide across the greasy-slick floor, her puffy tail like a rudder in the wind.

Even the spiders helped to interrupt Mom's boredom. Spinning their kaleidoscope webs across the window, they mesmerized Mom with their patience and creativity. Their glossy creations helped filter the sunlight and create a hazy softness that offered Mom a respite from the stark reality of her bleak surroundings.

From time to time the birds and squirrels would pass by the window and tweet or chirp or squeal a hello. And the spiders, in their quiet way, would also pass along their greetings.

The mice were very special, though. They were real friends, her very best friends, and they made her laugh, too (a rare experience for her).

When *The Humans* were getting along better they took great pains to replace broken windows and seal and paint the peeling house boards. Like Needles said, it wasn't like the house was impenetrable; after all he was a mouse, a professional. But why break into a fortress when you've got so many other opened castles in the kingdom?

When the siding began to fall away from the house-frame and the fence slats popped off the two-by-fours, it was like a neon sign, saying, "Comon' in" (at least that's what Needles said).

And that's when Mom's friends began to visit, and sure enough, it was easy pickin's. Things that used to be stored in reliable plastic containers were now just left opened on the table or thrown into the pantry. The mice squealed with joy when they discovered a delicacy left unsealed.

Mom loved it when *The Humans* discovered their invaded snacks. Mr. Granite, in particular, would bellow in horror. It grieved Mom to admit how much pleasure she experienced from seeing them in distress. It was a sad commentary on her life with them.

Mom suspected (or maybe just hoped) that perhaps Mr. Beaux had had something to do with the mice's recent appearance into her life, but then, maybe *that* was just wishful thinking.

When the weather was uncooperative, or when the birds or squirrels or spiders had other nests to feather, or nuts to hide, or webs to spin, and when there was fresh rat bait in the hallway, Mom returned to her life-long pursuit of chasing her tail. It was just a matter of time, she would tell herself. Just a matter of time.

But today she sensed a change. Dog lore was seldom wrong. That's why, when Mom obediently passed through the kitchen and down the hallway into her bleak room—she felt different.

She suppressed her anxiety as best she could, though all the while her mind raced with visions of phantom playmates invading her silent world. Thoughts of belonging to a real family (a family like Mr. Beaux's) peeked into her head. It was her version of the doggie lotto she imagined, as she quietly moved to a worn blanket, and waited for *The Humans* to leave for work. She surveyed her small world and wondered, what would her fate be?

Had it not been for the true blue norther, her day might have been just like all the others. But a true blue norther *had* come through and so today would be like no day before, and no day after. This day would change her life forever.

CHAPTER 4

More Chills for Feathers

Like most mornings, Mrs. Granite came to close Mom into the laundry room. She was as surly as ever. Her heavy smell (Mom said it was like the magnolia tree when it began to rot in late summer) preceded her into the small space. Quite predictably, she scowled as though Mom had committed some error in judgment just by being alive.

She didn't pet Mom's head, or pat her tummy, or scratch behind her ears. As a matter of fact, she didn't even touch Mom at all. Whenever one of Mom's soft hairs landed on her she would immediately pick it off and brush herself, as though a virus had settled onto an opened sore.

Humans say that dogs can tell when someone is uncomfortable in their presence, and Mom had no trouble identifying Mrs.

Granite's distress. It was clear that there would be no good omen coming from Mrs. Granite.

Mom felt sad, looking at Mrs. Granite for she stood there like an aging, overweight Bloodhound. Even on two feet she appeared too close to the ground. If she were on all fours, Mom thought, her chest would be dragging beneath her (as well as her jowls).

Like a Pomeranian who might have licked an electrical socket, her mousy brown hair stood out like geyser peaks blasting from her scalp. Tufts of it seemed to have petrified.

Experience and observation told Mom that when the Texas humidity penetrated it, Mrs. Granite's hair would turn into matted, gummy clumps, like a Retriever's coat might look after it slid through an oil slick.

Her face reminded Mom of a particular Poodle she encountered many years back at the dog-groomer. Subjected to the whims of her owner, like all animals, the Poodle was painted and sculpted and had ended up resembling a worn-out clown. Just like the Poodle, Mrs. Granite had two-inch nails painted with dark-colored enamel. Only now they were chipped and peeling, revealing layers of acrylic and glue. Mom was glad Mrs. Granite didn't touch her.

Autocratically bellowing out instructions to Mom, Mrs. Granite began to walk around the laundry room. She kicked several pieces of soiled clothing onto Mom's blanket. She didn't refill the water bowl or give Mom fresh food. She just had no interest. Mom couldn't remember the last time her bowls had been thoroughly cleaned. Mrs. Granite just poured new food over old and warm water over stale. As a final blow, Mrs. Granite turned to Mom and curtly said,

"Feathers, you're going to have a visitor today. You will have to be particularly obedient and not get in the way. You remember Mr. Jason? Well, I'm sure you do. Mr. Jason is coming by later this morning to get rid of those awful mice. Remember, Feathers, please do not get in his way...*this* time."

Mrs. Granite quickly closed the laundry room door and left for the day.

A shiver rolled down Mom's spine. Now she knew. A change surely was on its way, and it did not figure to be a happy one.

CHAPTER 5

Not all Memories are Good Memories!

Mom *did indeed* remember Mr. Jason. The first thing that came to mind was his smell—you know dogs have an excellent sense of smell. His was musty and stale. It reminded Mom of an old shoe that had been left out in the rain. He was a sloppy sort of man, too, shuffling when he walked, the way a lazy old Rottweiler does.

He was fat, like a pear, with rounded shoulders weighed down by his large belly. It stretched his shirt so tautly the last three buttons were perpetually popped. His thinning hair was combed straight back, but loose strands kept falling onto his face. Over and over, he'd scratch his head with his grimy hands, checking his ragged nails for dry scalp dirt. Mom was sure he had fleas.

On the one occasion that Mom had met Mr. Jason she tried to avoid his touch as best she could, but he made a point of running his damp, clammy hands through her silky fur. The worst thing, though, were his eyes. Mom said, when she looked into Mr. Jason's eyes she could see right through them, as though he had no soul. The pupils were dark and pinpointed, and he always squinted, causing the skin around his eyes to quiver and shake, like a crazed rat, just before it attacks.

They were evil eyes, Mom said, and she knew he meant no good. He was dangerous and she was afraid of him.

The shiver that ran down Mom's spine turned into bumps over her whole body. She began to shake and salivate, her tongue slightly extended, nervously lapping air.

He had only been to the house one other time, and Mom would never forget it. It was several weeks' back and he was working out of the laundry room making some kind of a mixture to get rid of the mice. Mom didn't know what kind of a surprise Mr. Jason was concocting for them, but it smelled very bad and made her eyes burn and fill with water.

While Mrs. Granite was away from the laundry room, Mr. Jason quietly turned to Mom and, staring at her with his rodent eyes, he began to smirk. He pretended to be nice, but animals know when evil is around and Mom was not fooled. She tried to back herself into the corner, snuggling her head into her tummy, hoping to protect herself from Mr. Jason's grip. But he persisted.

Slowly, with a plastic spoon in one hand, he got down on his knees and crept toward her.

"Feathers, Feathers, come on now, dearie. Have a little taste. It won't kill you. Not *this* time."

The closer he got to Mom, the harder she pressed her face

against her body. But the smell was so pungent she could hardly breathe.

Backed into the corner, having no place to go, her only hope was to get Mrs. Granite's attention. Mom never barked or whined, but she knew she had to do something. Mr. Jason made his final approach toward her and grabbed her by the neck, forcing her nose into the poisoned mixture.

"GOURUFF!" Mom bellowed.

Her heart and soul were in that plea, and she was sure Mrs. Granite would recognize it as a cry for help.

Mr. Jason dropped the spoon, and Mom's neck, and jumped to his feet. Mrs. Granite came running into the laundry room as Mom collapsed onto her back, her head falling to the side. Mr. Jason, composed by now, was wiping up the poison from the floor and talking sweetly to Mom.

"Oh, that's okay, Feathers. I know you didn't mean to trip me. It was my fault, clumsy old man that I am."

Mrs. Granite immediately began to scold Mom.

"Feathers, didn't I tell you to stay on your blanket in the corner? Here you are, making a mess...again."

Coyly turning to Mr. Jason, she began to apologize.

"Mr. Jason, I'm so sorry. She just can't seem to behave, lately. I just don't know what's gotten into her. Just push her over there with your foot, in her corner. She isn't very heavy."

She looked at Mom in disgust.

"I'm sure she'll stay out of your way, now."

Mr. Jason slyly looked at Mom with his quivering eyes, and replied, "Oh, no, ma'am, I'm sure it was my fault, old clumsy fool that I am."

Mom's attempt to limp to her corner was thwarted by Mr. Jason, as he jabbed at her with his smelly work boot, edging her into the corner of the room where she sat for the rest of the night, literally and metaphorically, licking her wounds.

That was several weeks ago. This time, Mom would be alone with Mr. Jason. Although terrified, she doubted that she would be able to muster up the strength and courage to cry out for help. Even if she did, who would hear her?

Part II

He was a coward to the strong:
He was a tyrant to the weak.

—Shelly
Rosalind and Hellen

CHAPTER 6

Mr. Jason Comes to Play

When Mom heard the kitchen door open she sank into her tattered blanket and rolled into a ball. Her body trembled. Her heart was pounding so loud and hard she could feel it in her ears; it was deafening, and she could barely breath. Tears were already welling in her eyes. She had no plan.

She dared not depend on Needles, Willie, and Bean. There was no way she could expect them to out-maneuver whatever diabolical trap she envisioned Mr. Jason laying out for them. There was nothing she could think of to save herself.

Yet, her mind raced with memories of the morning's magical wind and she would not allow herself to think that her end, at Mr. Jason's hands, would be the fulfillment of the omen.

Approaching the laundry room, Mr. Jason sounded like a

wailing tomcat.

"Feathers, F–E–A–T–H–E–R–S, guess who's here?"

Trying to control her convulsing body, she attempted to concentrate on Mr. Beaux, the dog next door. Thinking of him when she was in distress had become a spontaneous response. She was sure she heard his barks alerting the other neighborhood dogs to a delivery truck, or some other intruder. Or maybe he was growling at the new mailman, warning him to keep his distance. Whatever it was, she knew he was in charge!

His voice had given her so much comfort in the past, she hoped that thinking of it now would give her the strength she needed to foil Mr. Jason's malicious intent.

She began to reminisce about the nights when the moon was just right in the sky, allowing beams of light to stream into her small laundry room window. She listened to his Gouruffing for hours then, and, on clear nights, his *howl.*

She searched her memory to conjure up her one peek at Mr. Beaux. Was it a Collie he resembled? Was it a Doberman? Yes, a Doberman. No. No, not a Doberman! Perhaps a Great Dane? She couldn't get it quite right. What does it matter, she thought; they are *all* such *regal* creatures. He could be any one of them.

Mom fought her terror as well as she could. But alas—Mr. Jason was in the room. She could smell him.

He carried a small canvas bag, and even that had a foul scent (like a matted raccoon, fresh from the bayou, Mom thought). Trying to will herself invisible, she listened intently as he busily arranged his tools on the long worktable.

"La De Da De…Let's see. What do we have here? Yes, yes,

this is good. Oh, yes, oh yes. Four extra heavy-duty, hand-sharpened rat traps."

A droplet of blood appeared on the tip of his finger as he touched the razor-like wire stretched across the trap.

"Ouch," he winced.

Next he unscrewed a large glass jar filled with a milky white substance. As soon as the top was off the container, Mom recognized the pungent smell as the liquid Mr. Jason had tried to force her to lick a few weeks back.

"Poison," she thought.

As he examined the thick and syrupy liquid he murmured, "Excellent, excellent."

Looking further into his bag of tricks, he declared, "Oh, gracious sakes alive, what have we here? A little something for me? Yes, indeedy. A bag of cheddar cheese chips...Don't mind if I do."

He popped a chip into his mouth.

Mom could not hear all of his ramblings, but there was no mistaking it when he said her name.

"Feathers, oh my special *Feathers*.... De da de da de."

Mom lay on her blanket while the energy drained out of her like a stream of air slowly leaving a deflating tire. She thought about her life with *The Humans* and all her unlived dreams. No matter what, she thought, she was not going to give up without a fight.

BOOM. Like lightning. The reverie was over. *ZIP. KICK.* Mr. Jason was ready to play. He pulled the blanket from under Mom's body. Stunned, she rolled off onto the floor, while the dirty laundry she had been laying on flew in all directions. He aimed a dust-covered boot at Mom's face. Struggling to pull herself together, she ducked her head and scurried to the opposite side of the room. Mr. Jason was exuberant.

His lips, dry and crusted when he entered the house, were moist and slimy now. Like a drooling Saint Bernard, spittle gathered in the corners of his mouth. His yellowed teeth, gaping like an old bulldog's, grasped his lower lip and he bit down in fierce concentration. He wanted to get this right. He did not want to miss this opportunity to terrorize and torture Mom.

For the next few minutes, Mr. Jason toyed with Mom as she scurried away from him, running from one corner of the room to another. Finally, almost in boredom and with a look of disgust on his face, he grabbed her by the base of her ear and flung her onto the worktable. A sharp pain radiated down Mom's back. Her hearing was suspended and a low hum echoed in her head. A poker hot blast shot right through to all four of her limbs. Tingling followed a sudden numbness. Then, more hot surges.

A clump of hair stuck to Mr. Jason's hand as he grabbed for a sharpened rattrap, causing him to fumble with it.

"Damn," he muttered as he plucked furiously at the tufts of hair sticking to his hands. "Just keep the hell still, you mangy mutt."

His meanness was at its peak. Mom knew she was just too small to give any real resistance, but luckily Mr. Jason dropped the snapping mechanism to the floor. He shouted more threats at Mom.

"Stay still or I'll snap your skinny neck right now."

Then he went to work attempting to repair the guillotine.

With no place to go she obeyed his command, but continued to try and pull her thoughts together. Mr. Jason systematically plowed on. He retrieved a warm beer from his canvas bag, popped the metal top, and licked the overflowing foam from the side. Squatting on the floor, with his huge behind bulging from his sagging shorts, he firmly stuck the broken wire back into the wooden base of the trap, all the while eagerly guzzling his warm beer. After another can of suds and a hand-full of cheese chips, he began to mellow.

Mom silently lay on the worktable concentrating (and praying) with all her might to figure out a way to alter her fate.

Suddenly, as if out of thin air, three small figures appeared above her head, gingerly climbing behind the soapboxes on the storage shelf directly above her. She could see twitching noses and ears, and flicking tails. But she still felt as though she were sitting in a hollow cave, so she could not make out a word that Needles, Willie, and Bean were trying to say to her. She knew, however, that somehow they had managed to penetrate the barriers to the laundry room.

Mr. Jason, content for the moment with another beer and

even more cheese chips, continued to work at fastening the razor-sharp wire to the trap's wooden base. He was so engrossed with the task at hand he completely missed the activities of the mice as they strategically positioned the laundry products at the edge of the shelf, preparing for a direct frontal attack.

The buzzing in Mom's ears began to subside and she heard a high-pitched, but firm voice.

"Hey, hey, doll. Feathers. C'mon, wake up. Feathers? Hey babe, we need your help here, doll."

Mom listened intently.

"Feathers. Hey, Feathers. This is important. Try and focus now, we ain't got much time. Jason here is almost done with his repair job, and once the ol' bugger gets up again, we gotta move quick to get you outta this jam. We got a plan, but we're gonna need your help to carry it out. Now, c'mon doll, listen up, and get ready to GO GIRL."

At first, try as she might, Mom could not move. She could not seem to connect her thoughts to her body. Her terror had become so overwhelming that she had to separate herself from it. It was as though she had left her body on the table and become an observer of the horror she was experiencing. She could hear and she could see, but she could not respond to Needles' commands. She was paralyzed.

Turning over on his knees, Mr. Jason grabbed at the top of the worktable to help himself up. Fumbling along, trying to steady himself, his meaty paw landed on Mom's stiffened body. Feeling his clammy, greasy touch, Mom's soul jumped down from the ceiling and back into her body. With a renewed resolve she wiggled out from his hand. She got to her legs and pressed her backside into the wall. From above, the voice of hope again whispered.

"Good girl, that's it, doll, now you're up and around. We're half-way outta these digs already."

With hope back in Mom's body, her plumed bottom began to shake. In his drunken stupor, Mr. Jason was oblivious to the whirlwind of activity around him. Groping for some way to balance his bulk, he positioned himself between the dryer and a pile of storage boxes. He was a tub of oozing putty, like flubber, pouring himself into whatever space he pressed against.

Quite patient now, one by one, he slowly retrieved his death tools. Organizing his arsenal seemed to help him focus.

Needles, in charge like always, could tell that time was running out. Carefully crawling down the side of the wall, he continued to encourage Mom.

"Okay, Feathers, that's real good, doll. Keep on your feet. Keep movin'. We ain't got much time. Big boy over there is comin' back to life, and I predict he's gettin' a little tired of this game. My guess is he's gonna wanna get onto bigger and better things. Right, yous guys?" he said, turning to his two small compatriots. "Now listen up, here's what's gonna go down."

Needles explained the plan to Mom, while Willie and Bean kicked into action.

Straining to hear his every word, Mom could hardly believe what was happening. She just hoped and prayed that she would be able to act when the time came.

To reassure her, Needles flicked his long, smooth tail and gently stroked Mom's throbbing head.

"Hey, doll, you'll do fine. Me and the boys here, well, Bean ain't no boy, but, anyway, we're gonna get you outta this mess. All you gotta do is keep Jason distracted. Then, when we give you the high sign, follow Willie there outta this joint. That's all there's to it, babe."

Quickly looking from side to side and up and down, Needles scurried back up the wall almost as quickly as he had come down. As soon as Needles disappeared, Mom began to feel a hollow, empty sensation in the pit of her stomach. She thought she might throw up, except she knew there was nothing in her tummy to bring up. Trembling in the corner, but ready to act, she began to pant while a slight quiver started at the tip of her nose and gradually worked its way down to her tail. Her angular feet would not stay still. She felt like she was standing on four short noodles.

Like a pit bull preparing for the kill, Mr. Jason had finally steadied himself and again, his mood began to sour. He was losing his buzz and some fatigue was setting in. Forcing his eyes to focus on his prey, he was anxious to experience the pleasure of his hunt. Mom sensed a move was about to be made.

She knew she and her friends were outsized, but she prayed they were not outsmarted. Mom had heard tales of dogs (and other animals, like Mr. Jason), who for the fun of it targeted the smallest animal in the pack. Sometimes they zeroed-in on the injured ones reveling in their weaknesses. But, today hadn't been as much fun as Mr. Jason had expected. Instead of cowering, Mom was fighting back.

Mr. Jason's irritation was evident. He crushed the beer cans beneath his feet and kicked at the scattered clothing littering the floor. Grabbing at the jar of opened poison, he knocked the container against the back wall and a glob of the gooey solution landed on the vinyl worktable. A small cloud of gas rose toward the ceiling, as the liquid sizzled on the tabletop.

Anxious to get this over with, he activated the rattrap and set it near the poison-pond. The interaction of the gooey solution and the plastic tabletop intensified the odor, which had begun to seep throughout the room. The strong scent hit Mom and Mr. Jason like a brick, causing him to *almost* lose his balance. Unfortunately, it made Mom so nauseous she was not able to avoid his grasp.

With her neck firmly in his grip, Jason deliberately pushed Mom's nose closer and closer to the trap. Mom said she would never forget his obvious pleasure at her terror. His sounds and actions were almost impossible for Mom to describe. Animals, especially smart ones like Mom, learn to distinguish the sounds and actions of many different species, if they are to survive. But Mom said Mr. Jason had crossed the line from human to something else. Mom could not tell what breed of man or animal he had become.

He pushed her up to the trap and then away from it. He rolled her over on her back, reinforcing his dominance, and dropped small dots of poison on her exposed, soft belly. The burning sensation was unbearable. Little red welts arose on Mom's pink skin. All the time Mom was trying to remember Needles' instructions.

"Keep moving. Don't make it easy for him. Don't look into his eyes. Remember, he is just a bully and a coward" (but of course, he had become more than that). "Once our plan goes into effect, he'll fold."

(Mom could only hope.)

Keeping her faith, Mom repeated Needles' words over and

over to herself, like a mantra; she resolved to wiggle and shake as hard as she could. She wanted so much to believe the plan would work, but little by little she again felt her energy waning. She did not know how much longer she could continue to fight.

Finally, and none too soon, there was a stirring in the room. It was too subtle for Mr. Jason's ears, but Mom could hear Needles' voice.

"Okay, babe, time's almost here. We got just one more little detail…."

Mom began to prepare herself for the most important moment of her life. Just as planned, she stopped her fighting and wiggling and let out a huge sigh of resignation. Her body had become as limp as a wet rag.

Mr. Jason was ready, too. With a deadly grin he pulled Mom up to his face and said, "Well, I guess our little Feathers here has had enough. What'd ya say, cutie, how about a haircut."

She could feel his death grip as she dangled by her throat, his pinpoint eyes looking straight into her face. His pupils began to widen and his eyes blinked wildly. All the time, his skin was quivering. It was now or never.

Needles flicked his tail like a whip, and right on cue, Mom straightened her body and became as stiff as a beaver's tail. She looked directly into Mr. Jason's eyes, and from deep within her being, produced a low, deep, grumbling growl. (To this day she does not know where it came from.)

Using all the strength that her small body could muster, she lunged forward and bit down on Mr. Jason's bulbous nose. As bad as it tasted, she would not let go until he released her.

Now it was Mr. Jason's turn to yelp. With his nose pinched between Mom's cuspids, he could only make an airless, muted howl. It was music to Mom's ears.

Mom crashed to the ground, and Mr. Jason clawed at his bleeding face.

"*Blood,*" he wailed.

And then, a whimper.

"You've made me bleed. *That's not fair.*"

At that moment, Mom knew the spell had been broken. Mr. Jason was a human again, a pathetic human.

Out of his death-grip, Mom followed Willie and raced out of the laundry room, down the long narrow corridor, into the kitchen. She was delighted (albeit somewhat surprised) when she hit the sealed, dilapidated doggie door with so much force that it practically jumped from its rusted hinges. Willie just squeezed through a small crack in the wall.

Before returning to the laundry room to help the other mice, Willie escorted Mom to a group of outdoor neighbors who were busily working on another relic. An old common gate, chained and unused for years, was being "unchained" by a force from the adjacent yard. Mr. Beaux's yard. The plan was working.

CHAPTER 7

Mr. Jason Sees a Ghost

Willie high-tailed it back to the laundry room, just in time to join Needles and Bean with Mr. Jason. A small furry blur flew by Mr. Jason's face and knocked the bleach bottle right on his head. At the same time, Willie ran up Mr. Jason's leg and dug his razor-sharp claws into his thigh; he even gave him a little nip, just for good luck.

Needles scurried around the misplaced baskets and climbed up the wall, knocking over the opened bottle of liquid soap resting on the side of the washer.

Mr. Jason was in shock. His eyes were swollen and red as he rubbed at them, and even poured a warm beer over his head in an effort to rinse away the slimy residue. He blinked furiously, attempting to survey the room for his adversary.

"Where are you, anyway? What's goin' on? Come out and fight like a man," he blithered—all the time slipping and sliding in the sea of blue slimy soap and bubbling bleach.

Needles, Willie, and Bean had one more surprise for Mr. Jason. A grand finale, so to speak.

Giggling in a corner, watching Mr. Jason's antics, they came across a thin, worn, white sheet. What fun it would be, they thought, to really give Mr. Jason the fright of his life.

Each of the mice took hold of a corner of the sheet and slowly climbed to the top of the washing machine. Bean, the most agile of the three, jumped to the shelf above, her corner of the tattered sheet in tow.

Just when Mr. Jason's vision began to clear, and he seemed to get his bearings and steady himself, the mice jumped from their respective perches, simultaneously emitting a high-pitched squeal. The sheet flowed behind them, creating the illusion of a whining, ghost-like spirit, flying through the air.

As the mice let go of their makeshift poltergeist, the sheet fell over Mr. Jason's head. He scrambled and pawed at it in terror, gulping air and screaming hysterical incantations, trying to conjure up his own magical powers.

He bumped into the doorframe and bounced back into the worktable, all the time tugging at this mystical opponent.

Needles, Willie, and Bean savored the view of Mr. Jason as he finally rid himself of the sheet and practically flew from the laundry room, exiting the house, leaving all of his equipment behind. When he climbed into his old truck, the mice gave out one final sigh.

They looked at each other with pure delight. They had completed their mission.

"Hocus-pocus," Needles snickered to his two compatriots. "Let's boogie."

CHAPTER 8

More Magic in the Air

Mom was still on her side of the ancient old gate, responding to the instructions of the dog on the other side of the fence. Mom knew it was Mr. Beaux that she was listening to. She had heard his barks and howls and GOURUFF so many times in the past there could be no doubt. Just the thought of putting a face with that voice was enough to keep her going.

"Ack Ack Ack," Mr. Beaux commanded.

Mom knew that meant, dig, dig, dig, and dig she did. Other sounds told her to push, pull, and most importantly, *just keep up hope.*

It seemed to Mom that the whole neighborhood was involved in her rescue. Two large blue jays, which Mom had seen from her laundry room window, helped supervise the digging by giving progress reports (from a bird's eye view) to Mr. Beaux.

"Beaux, slightly more to the left. You'll have to remove that lump of dirt, away from the pole. Chirp, chirp (yes, yes, that's it). And, Feathers, you're doing great. Almost done, keep up the good work. (Tweet, Tweet, Tweet)."

Several hundred ants swarmed the old gate, nibbling at a sagging, rusted chain.

Three squirrels busily excavated large chunks of dirt resembling hardened nuts.

"GOURUFF. GOURUFF," Beaux cried out, and at once, everyone cleared away from the old gate as it came toppling down. Beaux immediately jumped across the new pathway and stopped dead, directly in front of Mom. There was an immediate silence as they stood, staring in each other's eyes, for the very first time.

The ants, forming a covey, emitted a high-pitched sound, imperceptible to the human ear. The blue jays chirped a "HALLE-LUJAH and AMEN." And one of the squirrels (the female) quickly brushed a tear from under her eye. (The two males just rapidly blinked and scurried away).

Mom, still somewhat in shock from her narrow escape, took a deep breath and spoke in a shaky voice.

"You must be Mr. Beaux. I would have recognized you any-where."

Mr. Beaux, behaving as though he had encountered a ra-bid pit bull, *froze*. He could not remember the last time he felt such terror. A small squeaky noise, sounding something like a "guf," was all he could muster from the depths of his throat. In desperation he jerked his head and mo-tioned for Mom to follow him.

They navigated the path across the gate where he led Mom to the far side of his yard, out of the view of the decimated fence. Once deep in his own territory his confidence began to return.

"There, there, Feathers. You'll be safe, here. Come now, sit in the sun where you can get rid of those awful shivers."

Even away from her yard and out of harm's way, Mom could not relax.

Everything was happening so fast. She just didn't know how to feel. At first she felt ashamed for being so frightened. After years of being blamed for so many things, she felt guilty.

"What will *The Humans* say?" she cried. "What have I done now?"

With her pleading, soft brown eyes, she looked up at Mr. Beaux, hoping for reassurance, but not knowing what to expect.

"Just stop that kind of talk. It makes me angry to hear it," Mr. Beaux exclaimed. "You've done nothing wrong. Mr. Jason is the culprit, and the Granites, too. They were supposed to protect you from him. *It's their fault.* Not yours!"

Putting his nose very close to Mom's, almost touching it with his own, he looked into her anxious eyes. With a voice as warm and gentle as the summer breeze, he said, "They let you down, Feathers. They have let you down for years. I don't want you to talk that way again. Not in front of me. I just won't hear it."

It was the most loving admonishment Mom had ever received. No one had ever before said that things were not her fault.

Shifting his attention back to the rampage across the yard, Mr. Beaux slowly slid back on his strong, muscular hind side, front feet straight, and his head erect. Mom, sensing it was a time for silence, stretched her delicate body out next to his.

She knew now that there had been no need for Mr. Beaux to acknowledge her earlier greeting. The dog whose howls and barks and bays she had been listening to for many years had been a part of her heart for just as long, and quite naturally, she understood she could never be without him again.

They sat, almost motionless. Mr. Beaux, tall and erect, like a commander, his ears rotating to pick up every sound of the skirmish raging on. Locating and identifying each of the warriors with his keen senses, he knew the battle was nearing an end when he heard Needles, still in the laundry room, calling out the final details of their plan. Mom sat safely next to him.

When Mr. Beaux heard Mr. Jason's wild ravings, he whispered, as if to himself, "all bark, all bark." Mom was not quite as assured. The cries and whimpers, the incantations, caused her fear to return.

Only when Mr. Jason's protests subsided and the sputtering of his old pickup faded did Mr. Beaux's ears soften and he knew they had achieved their immediate goal. They had defeated Mr. Jason and saved Mom, at least for the moment.

The entire brigade, the ants, the squirrels, the birds, and even the almost silent spiders stopped in their tracks. There was a deafening silence. But just for a moment.

In triumph Needles, Willie, and Bean came bounding from the battlefield, anxious to describe the scene in the laundry room.

Talking over each other in excited bursts, the mice reenacted Mr. Jason's predicament as he slipped around on the slimy floor trying to grab hold of his invisible challengers. Like a television script they reported their story.

Needles: "Like the time we was nibbling away at the sandwiches those bozo workmen brought. Remember, they saw us in their lunch boxes and came barreling down the ladders, only to fall over their cement buckets and water bottles, and each other. What a hoot. Well, this was better, cause I actually liked those guys—it was just a matter of a professional pride, you know, seeing an open lunch box. But this, this was a matter of survival.

"Yeah, that old Jason was bubbling and boiling with all his clothes turning colors like oak leaves during the autumn frost, his pants was like a patchy drab green and a mushroom brown, uggg."

Willie: "The bleach splattered on his grubby gray face, and those bright red oozing things popped up, like the time we outsmarted those rats and led them to the bin outside the Chinese laundry. Boy, those rats are dumb. I guess the meaner the dumber. That sure fits Jason."

Bean: "He was rubbin' and rubbin'—strugglin' to wipe away the mixture. He only managed to create more bubbles everywhere—his ears, his nose, the corners of his mouth."

And then in unison: "He was a bubbling baboon."

Needles said Mr. Jason grew very angry, breathing fast and turning around trying to find someone, *something* that had done this to him. "He was grabbin' in the air, grabbin' at the bubbles. He never saw us, but he'd grab in our direction, swearing, foaming at the mouth. Whew, what a sight!"

"Then he tried to stand up, but the floor was too slippery." Needles, Willie, and Bean laughed so hard at the memory of Mr. Jason's fumbling that they had to stop talking for awhile and go for a bathroom break. This caused Mom and Mr. Beaux a great amount of pleasure, laughing right along with them. It was the tonic they all needed.

When they returned, Willie continued the story.

Just as excited as in the beginning, the junior member of the trio described a beaten-down Mr. Jason.

"You should'a seen him...once he discovered there was no one around to blame and he began to look at the mess in the laundry room. His eyes got really big and he began to mumble to him-self, 'oh nnno, oh nnno. What have I done? What—wh—what am I gonna do?'

"That's when we got the idea of the ghost thing." (Beaux had to admit he particularly liked that touch!). "We was all hidden un-der this old tattered sheet. We was laughin' so much it was sort of jumping up and down, you know, like flying by itself. So, Needles, he was lookin' out and saw Jason watchin' the jumpin' sheet, real scared-like, so he says, let's give ol' Jase a big thrill. That's when we decided to make the sheet fly through the air, and look like a spirit, you know, like a ghost sort of.

"That's when he lost it. He was saying some kinda crazy prayers or somethin'—leapin' around...."

Bean gave Mom the biggest shock of all when she told of Mr. Jason's pitiful retreat from the house.

"What a pathetic creature. He reminded me of those sad look-ing bears the circus brings into town once a year, you know. We've seen them when we go near the railroad tracks to try and get some food scraps and other droppins.

"There he was trying to stuff his traps and poison and cheese chips into that smelly old bag, and he starts to whimper. Can you believe it? A grown man, crying. Squirming around. Throwing his hands up in the air, and practically blinded with bubbles pouring out of his eyes. Pretty soon, he just sank back and cried like a baby. Like one of those howling bears when they take away their honey to make 'em jump up on those painted boxes.

"Finally he just dropped his stuff in his tracks and high-tailed it out of there. I'll tell ya, I thought the old fart sprouted wings.

"We stayed right on his tail though, watchin' him stumble and fumble trying to get to his broken-down truck, nose still running, shoulders shaking. He couldn't even get his pickup outta here without a problem. It jerked up and back, rolling over the sidewalk, when he finally straightened it out he practically wiped out the mailbox!"

"Poor sucker."

They all started to laugh—Bean rolling her eyes, Needles standing back, throwing up his head, making squeaking sounds, like mice do when they know they've done a good deed. And Willie, beside himself, was rolling on the ground.

Mom and Mr. Beaux, already looking like an old married couple, watched each other through the corner of their eyes as they took in the mice's rendition of Mr. Jason's comic escape.

Fatigue seemed to come to everyone at once, and finally the laughter trailed off. Mr. Beaux looked at Mom and spoke quietly.

"Of course, Feathers, you shouldn't be surprised at all, because what Mr. Jason did is what all bullies do. When their intended prey call their bluff, they inevitably show their true colors and run for cover. Bullies are the biggest cowards of all."

CHAPTER 9

Mr. Beaux and Feathers
Share Their Worlds

With the ensuing quiet came reflection. A bright flash of reality pierced Mom's mind. There were no dog words (or human words she had ever heard), to express her emotions. Yes, she knew she loved Mr. Beaux and that she wanted to be with him forever. She also knew that it was not within her power (or any dog's) to make that happen. And, she was keenly aware of the retaliatory nature of those who had the power to do so.

So much had happened, and yet she knew, there was so much more to come.

With thoughts such as these swimming in her head, she vowed to concentrate on the here and now. Not knowing what the future would hold, or when her time with Mr. Beaux and her new friends would be over, she would make the most of the time she had. She would not regret this day.

Bringing her thoughts back to the here and now, Mom simply looked into the eyes of Needles, Willie, and Bean, and said, "Thank you, my dear friends. I owe you my life."

Speaking for the group, Needles replied, "Think nothin' of it, doll."

And so, as mice tend to do, he and his sidekicks stealthily disappeared as quietly and quickly as they had earlier arrived, a lifetime ago, to Mom's defense in her laundry room cell.

Alone with Mr. Beaux, Mom began to feel alive, but anxious. His voice gave her bumps, like when she heard Mr. Jason's name. But this was different. When she looked at him her heart beat faster. Like when *The Humans* used to give her a treat. But this was different, as well. When he barked at unknown visitors, or good friends, or at anything at all, she got nervous, like when she had to go to the vet for her shots. But this was even different from that.

This time, Mom was not scared or hungry or anything of that sort. This time, Mom was in love.

Mr. Beaux seemed to be gazing at Mom in a most peculiar way. His deep brown eyes penetrated her heart. He had a funny way of tilting his head and leaning toward her when he was listening, as if he rested on Mom's every word. He was magnificent. Mom told me that even though I have her beautiful fluffy hair and distinctly angular curved front legs (and the front paws of a purebred Pekinese), I have my Dad's length, strong nose, and of course, his beautiful deep brown eyes. And it was from both of them that I got my spirit.

As if noticing each other for the first time, Mr. Beaux spoke up.

"Feathers, how foolish of me. You must be exhausted and hungry. Please, come rest on my cushion and have a drink of cool water. Let me share my food with you. After you've had a little nap I'd like to learn more about you, and then maybe I can introduce you to some of your neighbors. It's going to be a long day."

Oh, my. How he loved her.

Mom followed Mr. Beaux to a cool area on the side of the house. It was surrounded by trees and there was an outdoor, weatherproof fan blowing ever so lightly. Placed out of the rays of the sun, Mom recognized the large dark cushion with Mr. Beaux's name and the embroidered heart on it. Just as she remembered, there was his water bowl collecting fresh, cool water throughout the day. It was no mystery to Mom why his family loved him.

After she had a long drink and a few bits of fresh food, Mr. Beaux offered Mom a very dainty piece of rawhide to chew on. He pulled the small piece off of a larger chunk, which he himself usually chewed.

"Well, thank you so very much, Mr. Beaux. The activity certainly has made me hungry, and tired too, but I just don't know how I am ever going to be able to repay your kindness, and to continue to take your hospitality, well, it seems very unfair."

Looking at Mom, he said, "Feathers, friends don't have to repay each act of kindness. If you're friends, then over time, it all evens out. You could do one thing for me right now, though, and that is to call me Beaux."

"All right then, Beaux," she said, and with that, Mom nuzzled her nose deep into Beaux's cushion, sinking into the scent of his body, for a long overdue nap.

Beaux, too, ready for his afternoon break, stretched out on the cool grass a little distance away from her. As they dozed off, Mom could see him looking at her with the kindest smile she had ever seen. With that vision in her head, she attempted to replenish her spirit for what lie ahead.

CHAPTER 10

Getting to Know Him

Already in tune with each other, they woke simultaneously and stretched and shook, and sniffed in the late summer air. There was no sign of the early morning blue norther, and, for a moment, the dramatic events of the day seemed like a distant dream. As natural as rain on a pond, Mom began to follow Beaux around the yard to meet and learn about her new outdoor neighbors.

The grass was cool and soft and when she looked closely, she could see ants and spiders scurrying around, busily going about their life's work. Mom never felt so alive. There were beetles, and caterpillars, too. And across the yard under the house, Mom could see more mice and a large rat. Mom had never been aware of so many different living things. From time to time Beaux and one of the outdoor creatures would pass a glance, or otherwise acknowledge each other in animal parlance.

Beaux began to explain what all his outdoor neighbors did, how they lived and how they played. She saw rows and rows of tiny ants taking food to their queen. She learned about caterpillars and how they turned into butterflies. Beaux warned her about rats, which he said are bully mice. She met flying things, as well. Mosquitoes, bees, flies, and wasps. They all had jobs, things that they knew how to do better than anyone else. Beaux explained it all to her.

Throughout the rest of the day Mom and Beaux shared stories about their lives. They talked about the blue norther that had come through that morning and the effect it already had on their worlds. They wondered out loud, together, about the fulfillment of an omen the norther might have brought. When they were done, Mom felt as if she had known Beaux forever. Her old life was over. She might be forced to return to her laundry room cell, but she would never be a prisoner again.

Mom was happier than she had ever been, and knew in her heart that the morning's omen was going to be of good things to come…. Or at least, she prayed that it would!

When she thinks about that day, even though terrible things had happened, it was also one of the most wonderful days of her life. She has tried to teach me that just because bad things can happen, good things can follow, too, and we must never give up hope. "That day brings back wonderful memories to me," she said. "And memories are treasures you keep in your mind for the rest of your life." Now you can see why my Mom is so smart!

CHAPTER 11

What It Means When the Sun Goes Down

Mom never got to spend a whole day outdoors, so she didn't know how to judge the time by the sun, but Beaux was so smart he could tell when different things were going to happen just by looking at the sky. That afternoon the sun was large and round and sat high the heavens. It was surrounded by a clear, cloudless blanket, stretching far beyond Mom's view.

Mom thought it strange that a short time ago the sky seemed to be falling in on her whole world, but now it was inviting and seductive. Even with the norther it had turned into another dog day, but the fan created a refreshing breeze, making it cool and very comfortable, especially in Beaux's special spot by the side of the house, on his soft cushion.

Beaux had become quiet and pensive. He seemed very concerned, and even a little agitated. Perhaps he had had enough of Mom, she thought, and wanted his cushion to himself. She stood up, ready to leave.

"Beaux, I apologize for taking up so much of your time, but I'm not sure what to do. I guess I'll just have to wait until *The Humans* get home to let me back in my house. I don't know how long that will be so maybe I should just go under the fence and wait by my back door so I won't take up any more of your time."

Beaux immediately became alert and rushed to Mom's side, touching her nose with his. It was Mom's first kiss. She was stirring inside.

"No, Feathers, I don't want you to go back to your yard. Not now, not ever. But, I'm afraid by the way the sun looks, you're going to have to go home soon."

Pointing toward a cluster of incoming clouds threatening to remove the sun from their view, he continued.

"If you look in the sky, you can see that the clouds are chasing the sun, and once they catch it and the shadows begin to fall, my family and yours will be coming home."

His voice began to crack and he quickly turned his face away from Mom's.

Now dogs and people have a lot in common. Really, all of God's creatures have a lot in common. They all feel pain, and they all feel joy. They all long for a gentle touch and they all want to share their lives with someone who will make them feel special and loved.

But, of course, there are lots of differences as well.

With her heart pounding rapidly, Mom knew she had to make the most important decision of her life. It was her time; she knew she was in heat. She had always dreamed of having puppies, and even Mrs. Granite had talked about Mom "producing income" someday. Mom knew that for Mrs. Granite, it would be to make money, not for love. Now, it would be for love.

Mom lifted her paw to Mr. Beaux's jaw. She slowly turned his face to hers, looking straight into Beaux's eyes.

"Beaux, I'd like to take a nap with you. Will you come with me?"

Knowing her situation, Beaux said, "Feathers, you know what this would mean. Are you sure this is what you want?"

The silence between them answered his question. They leaned into each other for support as much as for the closeness it offered.

The sun moving across the sky cast a purple shadow, like a curtain of protection, giving Mom and Beaux the privacy they needed to express their love for each other. Mom knew the risk she was taking, but she had no regrets. In her heart, she had known him for years.

They lay down together, savoring each other for as long as they could, listening to the sounds of the earth and the sky. When they were done they both agreed their love was the fulfillment of the omen. From that time on, Mom said Mr. Beaux was my Dad.

As Dad predicted, when the trees covered the sun, all sorts of things began to happen. It was the end of the workday and Dad's human Mom, BJ they called her, came home first.

As was BJ's habit, her first priority was to check in with Dad and get a report on his day's activity. Her strong voice preceded her as she approached the yard.

"Beaux! Hey, big boy, how was your day? Any strangers try and get past you?"

Dad always met BJ at the back gate. And, with his head high, and eyes bright and sharp, her questions were answered.

"Everything is fine," his body language would tell her. But today BJ had to penetrate the yard to find Dad and when she did, his anxious movements gave a different report.

BJ found Dad protectively guarding a small ball of what appeared to be a jumble of lively feathers. When the feathers "jumped in fear" and Dad looked at his master with pleading eyes, BJ did what all good dog people do. She bent down and firmly rubbed Dad's ears, and assured him that he was a good dog and that she was there to help him in whatever way she could.

The first thing, of course, was to gather the nervous puff ball in her arms and try to make sense out of what the day's events had been.

As her eyes darted around the yard and at the broken fence, it did not take BJ long to come up with a scenario of what had occurred. Talking to herself as much as to Dad, BJ said, "Oh my, who have we here?" Looking at Mom's nametag, she remarked, "Why, it is a bundle of feathers. It sure is, I thought so. What a perfect name for a fluffy little dog," she exclaimed. Dad, of course, could not agree more. "Gouruff," he responded. "Gouruff, gouruff!"

BJ was not big nor was she small. She was just Dad's human, and he loved her dearly. Her reddish blonde hair showed signs of shiny silver streaks, and was often drawn off her face with a brightly colored bandana. Her appearance was predictable. She was clean, not always neat, but she gave no thought to her dress, as long as it was functional. Today, like most days, she wore a pair of draw string pants and a tee shirt. She could be pretty when she needed to, but over the years she realized that beauty was an inner quality. If you let it grow from the inside, the outside would take care of itself.

She loved Dad for the faithful animal that he was, and had that special gift of treating all living things with love and respect. She could see no difference among God's creatures, and had little tolerance for those who did. She was smart and kind, too. Mom felt protected in her arms.

As BJ held Mom, she examined her and cuddled her at the same time.

"Oh, my precious little sweetheart. I must take care of that broken fence. And look at those welts on your little tummy. What could have caused that? And you seem so thin, hummmm! I just know your family is going to be worried sick when they find you missing."

She turned to Dad.

"Beaux, what a good boy to protect Feathers here. I do know that whatever it was that happened, you did the right thing. But now, we are going to have to figure out a way to get Feathers back home."

With that, Dad began to growl and bark and jump up and down, and Mom made a slight whimpering sound.

BJ was the kindest human Mom had ever met. After she straightened Mom's hair with her strong fingers, and brushed some of the dirt from her tummy, she gently placed her down on the cushion and spoke to her and Dad.

"I think you two better say goodbye now. I'll go and cover that hole under the fence. As soon as the Granites get home, I'll take Feathers back to her family. It will be better for everyone if they don't find you together."

BJ went over to the fence and began to fill in the hole that led to the Granites' yard. Now the sun was totally behind the trees and the soft breeze had just about stopped. The air was very still and it was almost impossible for Mom and Dad to breathe. They were both swallowing hard and they could not look in each other's eyes.

Dad was the first to speak.

"Feathers, I have never thought of running away from home, but I am sure if we planned it we could...."

Before he could finish his sentence Mom put her nose to his and, while trying to blink her tears away, she said, "My dear Beaux, you know that just wouldn't do. You are a watchdog, and you have a responsibility to your family. And, you know how possessive and mean *My Humans* are. They would do everything in their power to get me back, just because they knew I wanted to leave. No, no, we'll just have to bide our time, and pray for the best. When BJ comes back and takes me home, I don't know when or how I will ever see you again. But I promise you this. I will. I know the blue norther carried a message for us. We must figure out how to make its promise come true. *We must!*"

BJ turned from the fence toward Mom and Dad. Mom gently rubbed Dad's nose one last time. She slowly walked away from the cushion they shared and met BJ in the middle of the yard. Feeling weak and heartbroken, Mom stumbled. Dad began to lunge toward her, but with one look from BJ, he understood he would only make things harder for Mom, and turned away and went to the side of house. He could not bear to see Mom leave. BJ picked Mom up

CousCous Mackey

one last time and carried her to her home, gently caressing her body, and humming a soothing gentle tune.

Dad could not speak. When he tried to bark, only a deep howl came out. Many of Mom's new friends, knowing that the time for her to go home had come, began to make soft, whining noises. No one could actually speak any words. For that whole evening and the next and the next, Dad could only do the most basic elements of his job. He could not imagine life without Mom. His heart was broken.

Part III

We did not dare to breathe a prayer
Or give our anguish scope
Something was dead in each of us
And what was dead was hope.

—Oscar Wilde
The Ballad of Reading Gaol

CHAPTER 12

Why Can't Humans Learn to Listen?

Standing at the front door with Mom in her arms, BJ could hear a loud commotion in the house.

"Feathers. Feathers!" Mrs. Granite shouted, "Where are you? What's happened in this laundry room? It's a terrible mess. I want to know what happened *now!*"

Looking toward the ringing doorbell, Mrs. Granite saw BJ holding Mom in her arms. She opened the door and immediately grabbed Mom away. Shaking her, she cried out, "What have you done? The laundry room is a mess."

Mom, still in a deep blue mood, was abruptly brought back to reality. She was accustomed to harsh treatment. Still, it never ceased to renew her feelings of humiliation and anger.

"It's a good thing Mr. Granite won't be home until tomorrow night. I'll have to clean up this mess before he gets back. Don't think I'm going to let you off the hook, young lady. You're going to have to take care of yourself. There will be no treats tonight, and maybe not even dinner."

Putting her at arm's length, as through she was a dirty dish-cloth, she continued.

"Oh, just look at you. Your hair is all matted and you have dirt all over your coat. Where in the world have you been? Have you been playing with that dirty mongrel next door?"

The door was wide open and Mrs. Granite's ranting could be heard over a long distance. She shouted her displeasure at Mom for the entire world to hear. From BJ's backyard deep growls could be heard. Several of the more mobile neighborhood creatures began to gather at Mrs. Granite's porch. A swarm of mosquitoes nestled in her gummy hair, and three flying spiders settled themselves at the base of her neck, ready and *hoping* to strike at a moment's notice.

Having heard enough, at last BJ interrupted. Her heart told her to shake some sense and manners into Mrs. Granite, but, for Mom's sake, her head settled her down.

"Err, hello, Mrs. Granite, uh…Gladys. I'm very sorry to bother you, but I found your beautiful Feathers outdoors when I came home today. She is such a good girl that I can't imagine what fright-ened her so to drive her from her home."

Mom tried to lick Mrs. Granite's nose to say hello and let her know she hadn't done anything bad. But like a lot of humans, Mrs. Granite ignored both BJ and Mom. Her mind was made up, with-out hearing the whole story.

Mrs. Granite gave BJ an agitated look and attempted to slam the door in her face. BJ put her shoulder to it and held her ground.

"You know, Mrs. Granite, if Feathers ever becomes too much for you, we have a large yard and would be more than happy...."

Before she could finish her sentence, Mrs. Granite shoved the door with all her force, leaving a frustrated BJ alone on the porch.

CHAPTER 13

First Things First

Many things in her life had changed, but the laundry room was just as it had been for the last several seasons: bleak, cold, and full of refuse. Mom felt desperately alone. There was so much to share with Dad. And, she needed his support more than ever. Try as she might, she knew her spirits were waning. She attempted to concentrate on happy things and better times, but her mind raced.

She thought about the true blue norther and all that it had brought her. She concentrated on her time with Dad and what their sharing would bring into their lives. She had hoped that they might have a litter, even a small one, but her nourishment had become so infrequent and so meager, she wondered if she would have even *one* healthy puppy.

Refusing to give up hope, she fantasized about puppy names and planned out lessons she would teach their baby. She mused about how wonderful it was to have met Dad and all her other new friends. She thought about the beauty of just being a Mom. The hardest thing, of course, was trying *not* to think.

Dad, on the other hand, could hardly think at all. He had stopped his hourly patrols of the family property, allowing a deliveryman to get all the way to the end of the driveway without a warning. All he wanted was to be with Mom.

Mrs. Granite took care of that. After cleaning up the laundry room she dragged the storage boxes into the yard and pushed them up against the sagging fence—but only after driving several deep stakes into the dirt. Mom would not get out of her backyard again.

There were occasional sightings, like during Mom's dwindling morning outings. Dad dared not do more than look, though, for fear of reprisal by the Granites. He was losing his grip. He had to pull himself together before he lost all self-respect. He had to start doing his job again, but how?

Mrs. Granite never told Mr. Granite the whole story about that very bad day in late summer. She was just glad that the awful mice were gone and chose to forget the rest of it.

Needles, Willie, and Bean, however, were not gone. They knew that they'd have to be very quiet and make themselves practically invisible if they were going to help Mom and Dad through this terrible time. And so they did.

Needles and Dad had been through a lot over the years, but Needles had never seen him such a state.

Burrowed into a small hole under the Granite's home, Needles lamented the situation.

"I don't mind telling you guys," he said to Willie and Bean as he nervously paced up and back. "This really scares a guy, you know, to see a big lug like Beaux in such a state. It ain't easy to think that I'm gonna have to take control of this situation without being able to depend on that big knucklehead."

Flicking his tail and wiggling his pointed nose, like he always did when he was agitated, he continued.

"WOW, we really gotta get in gear here. Things could be goin' down real quick. We gotta be prepared for the worst of it."

Willie and Bean watched in silence as Needles paced around the room in a constant state of energy. He wasn't a very big mouse, as mice go, but he was lean and smart. And even though he gave Dad credit for a lot of their coups, Needles was no slouch. He wasn't a purebred, I guess no mice are, but he was streetwise and he knew how to get things done.

Bean in particular liked to watch Needles. As smart as he was, though, he was just as dense as all males of every species were when it came to the obvious. Bean had had a thing for Needles for as long as she could remember. The problem was that he couldn't seem to stop treating her like a kid. He still thought of her as that skinny, shaggy lookin' little mouse that used to play around the neighborhood gardens and trashcans. Bean had tried to get his attention many times. Curling her tail. Slicking back her coat. Once she even played around with an old bleach bottle, trying to make herself a blonde. Nothing seemed to work. Needles just continued to tease her, often calling her the Bleached Beanster. She hated it, but finally just settled for being one of his sidekicks.

To Willie, though, they were just Needles and Bean. Anything more complicated went over his sleek head. All Willie cared about was a good meal and a place to sack out. No one really knew where he came from. Rumor had it some exterminators got his whole family when he was at school, trying to get a few crumbs out of the kids' lockers.

Anyway, he won't talk about it. He just showed up one day with not much else than his appetite. He was a little runt then but he was street-smart and fast and could get into cracks and crevices that Needles and Bean had long since outgrown.

While he hasn't gotten too much bigger, he's a whole lot smarter, and he's completely devoted to his compatriots. For the last few years they stayed together, taking care of each other and just trying to get along.

So there they sat, looking at each other. Needles paced, flicking his tail, and twitching his sharp pointed nose. Bean, grooming herself, looked at Needles. Willie watched them both, ready for their commands.

"Well," Bean said, taking charge. "I guess that doesn't leave us much time to dawdle. We'd better get started. First things first."

With that the three mice gingerly peeked out of their makeshift foxhole and scurried to Mom's cell.

CHAPTER 14

That's What Friends are For

When *The Humans* were gone during the day, seeing Mom was a piece of cake (it was not always such an easy task.) The sight of her, though, alarmed the mice. There was definitely a sharp decline in Mom's mood. She seemed to be getting more and more confused by the hour. She couldn't even make the simplest decisions, or manage the most basic tasks. Her appetite was all but gone, and she had stopped grooming herself. Mom was depressed.

Like all males, Needles was baffled and could only give her orders.

"Feathers, you gotta start eatin', doll. I mean, C'mon sweetheart. Things ain't that bad. You should just pick yourself up and get goin' again."

Willie just echoed Needles. "Yeah, Feathers, you shouldn't feel so bad."

Exasperated, Bean piped in, "Oh how typical. 'Just pull yourself together'," she mimicked.

Finally, Bean decided to bring some order to the situation.

"Needles, Willie, I hate to say it, but your male chromosomes have outdone your worthlessness on this issue. Don't you realize that Feathers *should* feel bad? Things are pretty awful right now for her and Beaux. And, Needles, she can't just 'pick herself up and get goin'. Where is she to go? How is she to go?"

Finally, Bean threw her head back and scrunched-up her little body from the top of her head to the tip of her tail. She shook and quivered and stretched back out to what seemed to Needles and Willie to be twice her size. Then she started to bellow out orders.

"Now hear this, *FIRST THINGS FIRST*. You brain trusts figure out a way to get Beaux into this yard to start seein' Feathers again. I know he can't come into the house, but there's got to be a way to get those stupid boxes out of the way. There's got to be more than one way to skin a cat." (An idea that held great appeal for all of them.)

Needles blinked his eyes several times, like he always did when he was thinking, and began gnawing on a piece of old packing. It was another sure sign that the gray matter was working.

"Well?" Bean prodded.

Needles gave Willie a high-paw and they headed out of the laundry room toward the backyard. Everyone remained clueless, except Needles, that is.

After they were gone, Bean turned her attention to Mom. She was a pitiful sight, lying on the floor looking years older. She was beyond tears. Deep heaves came from her chest, and a small amount of dribble had dried at the side of her mouth. Her eyes, usually a soft

CousCous Mackey

sparkling brown, were dull and half-hidden by fallen lids. Her perky, plumed tail, her trademark of elegance and sophistication, was matted and listless, clumped together like a ball of scrambled string.

Bean gently smoothed Mom's forehead with her tail, and spoke ever so softly in her ear.

"Oh, sweetheart. I know your heart is broken. This is the worst time in the world for you, and I can't promise things will get better anytime soon. But, maybe together we can start getting you back on your feet."

Bean's words were like a floodgate. They opened up all the emotions Mom had been holding in since the day Mr. Jason had come into her home and turned her world upside down. As she slowly rolled her head over, resting her chin on the soiled laundry room floor, tears began to stream down her face.

"Oh Bean, oh Bean," she cried, "What am I to do? *The Humans* have never been a warm family, but now it's worse than ever. Mrs. Granite hardly ever looks at me anymore, and she and Mr. Granite are arguing all the time. Just the other day he was yelling at her because the house was such a mess and he couldn't find any clean socks. He came into the laundry room and threw a fit when he saw all the dirty clothes piled up in the corner. He looked at me in disgust and told Mrs. Granite that maybe the laundry room was too crowded, and that something would have to go. I know he never wanted me in the first place. Once he finds out there is more than just me, I just don't know what he will do."

"Now, now, Feathers," Bean consoled her. "You know the whole neighborhood knows that the Granites have never gotten along. Why, Needles told me that just the other day, while running across the cupboard on his way to the laundry room, he heard Mrs. Granite yelling at Mr. Granite for never being home anymore, and accusing him of having a girlfriend. Can you imagine that jerk with a girlfriend? With his bony knees and pointed head? And what's with that new hairdo? I swear that if Needles' coat gets thin and he pushes it around like Mr. Granite does, I'll push him in a slick of hair remover."

Bean's efforts were taking hold. Mom couldn't help but laugh from this description of Mr. Granite, and managed to perk up a bit. Enough at least to start breathing a little easier and to focus her eyes.

"I know they have never been very close, Bean," she said lifting her chin off the dirty floor, "but at least Mrs. Granite used to stick up for me. Now, I am a total inconvenience to her, too. You and I both know they would never be kind enough to just throw me out. I don't care what happens to me, Bean, but I have at least one baby to think of now." She heaved a big sigh and dropped her chin back on the damp, sticky tile.

"Okay now, Feathers. You may be right. Maybe Mrs. Granite isn't going to protect you anymore, but we still have some choices to make. That is the best that we can do. Right now our first order of business is to get you back on your feet. We'll have to figure out the rest later. I know it isn't easy to eat at a time like this, but you have to promise me you will begin taking in some nourishment—and exercising—starting right now. No more lying in this musty corner all day."

"Oh Bean," Mom cried. "What would I do without you?"

"There, there, Feathers," Bean comforted. "That's what friends are for."

CHAPTER 15

Needles, Willie, and Bean

The laundry room was more congested than ever. Packing boxes littered the floor and odd pieces of furniture and broken bric-a-brac were strewn over the worktable, which Feathers could no longer reach. Her view of the trees and the birds and the squirrels was all but obliterated. She could still see the window itself and the face of anyone who might look into her cell, but no one was ever there—at least not so far.

While Bean and Mom talked about the options available to them, they could hear a commotion outside the window. Bean jumped up on the chipped sill to see what all the activity was about. She was beside herself with joy when she began to describe the scene to Mom.

After a tenacious search by Needles and Willie, they alerted

Dad to several loosened slats in the fence leading almost directly to the storage area outside the laundry room window. The area was not large, and it was only lately that the Granites had been piling up discarded trash, which weakened the rotted enclosure. The area was so small that the debris was piled as high as the laundry room window. Once Dad found the loosened slats, it was just a matter of time before he began his desperate push to penetrate the barrier.

Running up and back on the railing designed to keep the fence together, Willie beamed with pride at their triumph. Dad never looked up, but continued, head down, ramming the bottom of the loosened wood.

Bean peered out of the window and gave Mom a detailed description of the activity.

"Go for it Beaux, go for it!" She shouted. "It's Beaux and Willie, and I think I see Needles. Beaux is pushing through the fence. I think he's going to make it. He's almost through." She sounded like a frenzied announcer at a chicken fight.

Mom became alive again, whimpering and barking and making a fierce squeaking sound all at once.

"But Bean, what will he do when he gets through? How will we be able to see each other? I can no longer get to the window and I can hardly see it from the floor."

Scurrying around looking for something to help them out, Bean started knocking soapboxes to the floor.

"I don't know exactly what we're gonna do, but we'd better think of something quick, or that big lug of yours is gonna charge right through this wall. I have never seen such a determined look on his face. I know that if he doesn't get a glimpse of you after all this work, we'll have to put him in a cage! Quick, start pushing all those dirty clothes into the corner. Pile them on top of these soapboxes. You won't be able to get to the window, but you'll sure give him a better view of you."

In the midst of all the confusion, Mom stopped and looked plaintively up at Bean.

"Oh, no. Stop. I don't want him to see me like this. I look awful. I'm a total mess. Tell him to go away."

But before Bean could reassure her, Dad's magnificent head came into view. The veins in his muzzle and neck were extended and pulsating, and his tongue was lapping in the air. His taut body was precariously balanced on a perch of old fence slats, plastic trashcan pieces and broken-down furniture. His breathing was so hard and deep, it caused the window to becoming fogged. He lapped at it with his tongue, clearing off the mist.

Straining to see inside Mom's laundry room prison, his eager eyes met her face. Quivering with emotion and weak from her ordeal, Mom struggled to balance herself on the piled-up soapboxes and dirty clothes.

Neither of them said a word, yet volumes were spoken. The warmth of their love spread through the room, further clearing up the misted window. Bean, winking at Dad and mouthing a "job well done," gingerly jumped down from the sill and gently brushed Mom's face with her tail as she left the laundry room.

Needles and Willie, still elated over their feat, were jubilantly running up and down the broken fence slat when Bean came around the corner, shaking her head in disbelief. Frustrated, she commanded,

"Hey, you two lugheads, get outta there for a while. Let 'em be alone."

Needles broke in, "Oh, uh, yeah, uh, so okay then, pal, we'll be back in a little while. Take it easy up there buddy, I think you're pretty solid right now, but no heavy jumpin'. Come on then, Willie, let's get us a little siesta time. See ya later then, pal."

In a demanding voice, Bean repeated herself. *"Will you two just puleezze get out of there, NOW."*

CHAPTER 16

Love as a Tonic

Dad paid no attention to his friends. His eyes and ears were for no one but Mom. Settling himself on the piles of trash beneath the window, Dad looked longingly at her. Like always, when he was ready to hear her speak he tilted his head ever so slightly and cocked his ear in her direction.

Mom could hardly breathe, let alone say any words. She could only gaze at Dad with feelings ranging from bursting love to desperate despair. Mom knew their love could not conquer all.

Dad seemed to possess the power to read Mom's mind. So, lowering his eyes and turning his head, it was he who first spoke. "How beautiful you look, Feathers. Even with all your thoughts of despair and doom, you are as radiant as you were when I last held you."

No longer able to hold in her pent up emotions, Mom blurted

out, "Oh Beaux, I have missed you so much. What is to become of us? What is to become of our baby? I worry all the time about the Granites taking it away from us. Sometimes, not knowing what's in store for me, I think that maybe I should just end it all. Then I feel so guilty and sad I can't bear it. I'm so confused and frightened."

Mom melted into the pile of dirty laundry and strewn soap boxes, heaving sighs of hopelessness.

Dad waited patiently for Mom to recover. As he surveyed her surroundings his shame and anger were almost unbearable. Being a dog, he knew there was nothing he could have done. As an animal, he would always live at the mercy of humans. But, the very thought of Mom being trapped and isolated in her slowly decaying environment pained him beyond words. He was ashamed for the human race. He was angry at the Granites. Then and there, he made a silent vow that he would never abandon her again.

The stress on Mom had taken its toll, yet in Dad's eyes, Mom was as beautiful as ever. He could see the signs of the mental and physical strain. Several weeks pregnant and she had lost weight; clearly they would not be having a litter. Her hair, usually a billowy cloud, was knotted and dull, and her eyes, always sparkling and clear, were clouded. All signs of malnutrition.

It was all Dad could do to hold his thoughts of the Granites to himself. Just thinking of Mom's last few weeks made him sick.

Needles had been keeping a close eye on the house, reporting everything he heard and saw to Dad. Mr. and Mrs. Granite's relationship had deteriorated quite severely. Not wanting to alarm Mom, he didn't share everything he heard with her, but word had it that the Granites were planning to sell the house and move away, separately. It was anyone's guess what would happen to Feathers.

Mom *was* aware of the obvious disruption in the household. Mrs. Granite, never a warm and loving pet owner, had at least met her basic needs. The laundry room, where Mom slept and ate, *had* been orderly. Her food and water was not always fresh, but she never missed more than one meal, maybe two.

But all this was past. Mrs. Granite had been neglecting to provide Mom with even the basics. Her tattered pink cushion had been taken away weeks ago, in punishment for the incident with Mr. Jason. It seemed as though dealing with her own problems was all-consuming for Mrs. Granite, and that she had all but forgotten that Mom existed. Tending to Mom's needs had become just too troublesome.

Relying almost entirely on scraps Dad would have the mice sneak in, she thought about rationing her food. But with no appetite and all of her incentive gone, she could not muster the energy.

Mom's memories of Mr. Granite were no more pleasant. He had never taken any interest in Mom, except to issue warnings to Mrs. Granite about making sure Mom never made any mess, or caused any problems (which of course she never did). And most important, to make sure she never had any puppies. His warning to Mrs. Granite was clear. If Mom ever got into *trouble,* he'd solve it. His way.

When Mom first heard these harsh words they made her shudder, but now, with the reality of her baby on the way, the horror of what might happen was unthinkable. The pressure was there, and it was great. Except for the fact that Mom was shamed into relieving herself in the corner of the room, she was thankful that Mrs. Granite did not come around. On the few occasions she did come into Mom's cell, she looked more haggard and tired than ever. Mom just hid behind the washer. She had no way of knowing when, or how, things would change.

Change would come, though, and sooner than anyone knew!

Mom tried to put those memories behind her for now. It had only been a few minutes since Dad's face appeared in the laundry room window, yet Mom felt as though her heart was once again beating and bringing life to her and her baby.

Her venting subsided. She took a deep breath, and then another. She looked up at Dad and as though seeing him for the first time, a beautiful smile blossomed on her face. She began to laugh.

"Oh, my sweet Beaux, your love is such a tonic. It's so wonderful to see your face again. I dream of it every night and I imagine it when I lie here. Right now, it's more handsome and reassuring than any dream or fantasy I could ever conjure up."

Dad, being such a modest soul, swallowed hard, and fidgeted, almost losing his balance.

CHAPTER 17

A Dog's Life

Figuring the Granites would not return for several hours, Dad and Mom continued to visit through the laundry room window. Managing to stabilize his perch, he assured Mom and himself that he could easily return. He encouraged her to take a nap while he did his hourly patrol of his house. It was the first time in weeks that he felt like doing his job. And for Mom, the first time in weeks that she could rest peacefully, listening to Dad's barks and howls at passing neighbors and deliverymen.

Later that afternoon Mom awoke to Dad's contented gaze.

They both tried to avoid talk about the future. There were so many questions and concerns in their minds, but no solutions. There never were, when living at the mercy of others.

Dad turned his head and viewed the evening sky. They were

having an early fall.

"The time is passing quickly, Feathers...."

She interrupted him.

"Yes, yes, I know. The Granites will be home soon. But you know, Beaux, they never stay around for very long, so maybe you can come back later tonight."

The edge to her voice was unmistakable.

"I'm not thinking about this evening, my dear," Dad gently replied. "I'm thinking about the next several days. We both know that your time to deliver is coming."

Mom did not want to think about her time coming. There were too many unknowns that frightened her. Dad was frightened, too.

"Yes, I know I am almost due. I can feel at least one little puppy in me now. It moves and runs in the middle of the night. Sometimes I think we are going to have a Greyhound."

Dad let out a deep laugh and teased her about having a Greyhound uncle in his own mixed past.

"Really, Beaux, I'm not sure when our baby will come. My diet is off, and I've been so depressed...."

Her thoughts trailed off, and Dad knew there was nothing more to say. He understood that he could never appreciate what she was going through. He was beside himself with fear and anguish over their predicament, and could only imagine what her world had been like for the last two months. He knew he could never understand the feelings of a Mom-to-be.

"Well, Feathers," he said. "We'll talk more about this tomorrow. At least now we can see each other and visit and take each day as it comes, together. Being together is what's most important."

He bid Mom a good night and promised to return in the morning. Even though her room was a mess, he was glad that Mrs. Granite had spilled some food on the floor. Needles, Willie, and Bean, always on their toes, managed to gnaw a small hole in the rubber hose that connected the washer to the water outlet, providing a small drip of moisture for Mom's comfort.

"Goodnight, Beaux," Mom said, wishing with all her heart they had never had to learn what it meant to lead a *dog's life*.

Part IV

If there is no God for thee,
Then there is no God for me.

—Anna H. Branch
To a Dog

CHAPTER 18

Tuesday's Child is Full of Woe

Several days had passed since Dad was able to concoct a reliable way to visit with Mom through the laundry room window. His reports on her impending delivery filled the whole animal neighborhood with tension. Word spread the only way it can in this kingdom, with hisses and meows and barks and growls echoing for blocks around. Everyone was abuzz, hoping and praying for the new pup.

Monday morning, October the second, BJ encountered Mrs. Granite as they both were leaving for the day. Mrs. Granite was deep in her own despair. Her pasted-on Poodle nails had been bitten to the quick. Her sprayed hair was falling around her forehead and neck in matted clumps, and she was fat!

"Hello there, Mrs. Granite," BJ said, approaching her in the driveway. "How is that beautiful little Feathers of yours? We sure have missed seeing her. I hope she isn't still being punished for that incident way back in early August?"

Looking at BJ as though she was a total stranger, Mrs. Granite replied foggily while she piled herself into her car.

"Uh, uh, Feathers, oh yes. She's fine, uh, I think...Oh, I'm sure she's fine. You know, animals just seem to have a way of providing for themselves. Anyway, she'll be moving soon. That is, if my new apartment will let me bring her. If not, well, something will work out. We'll be moving by the end of the month. Yes, we have to be out of here by the end of the month, so something will work out...I guess."

With that she quickly backed out of the driveway and sped away.

BJ tried to rush to the car to get more information, but it was too late, and she knew time was running out.

October the third was a Tuesday, and it was on that woeful day that I was born. Dad continued to visit Mom as much as he could but almost magically strangers began to appear at the Granite home.

Real estate agents, guarding the house as though it were a fort, began to prepare it for showings. On one occasion, BJ tried to break in to steal Feathers away, only to be stopped by an agent who said they had received specific orders to keep "trespassers" off the property.

Another agent tried to repair the pried-away wooden fence slats that Dad and Willie had managed to loosen. Dad viciously charged the agent and called for Needles' help. Needles scurried up the fence trying as hard as he could to look like a rat. He bared his teeth, stretched his tail, and puffed up his hair. The agent, a woman, was undaunted by Dad, but the minute she saw Needles she screeched, jumped up on her tiptoes and ran away.

"Well, that's a job for the new owners," she exclaimed. "You can't cover all the bases."

When the agents went into the laundry room, Mom crawled behind the washer as far as she could. It was not easy, but she was determined to keep out of the way, at least until her baby was born. She had no illusions as to what would ultimately happen, but she drew strength from Dad and his courage.

Tuesday morning, the weather was unusually wet and dreary. Mom had been right last August when she predicted an early fall. The temperature was unseasonably low, and all the forecasts were for an early, hard winter. The good news was that the bad weather kept the real estate agents away for the day and gave Mom the privacy she needed to bring me into this world. Or at least into the laundry room.

Dad routinely came to see Mom as soon as the house was empty. It was almost impossible to rely on the Granites' schedule, so Dad had to be particularly careful. On this day he encountered Mr. Granite walking to his car. Dad was pacing, waiting for him to leave so he could visit Mom. Mr. Granite, the coward that he is, was annoyed at Dad's pacing and began to taunt him. Dad took great pleasure in snarling at Mr. Granite and producing a deep devilish rumbling growl, promising himself he would have a chance at Mr. Granite one day soon.

Dad finally made it to his perch, but Mom was nowhere in sight.

"What a morning this is turning out to be. Will nothing go right?" Dad exclaimed.

Continuing to scrutinize the trash-filled room, he thought he detected a subtle movement under a pile of dirty clothes and crumbled newspapers. It was as though someone had built a small fort. A little refuge. Like a bolt of lightning, it hit Dad. Had Mom needed to provide a nesting area for their new baby? Dad's anxiety level rose to its limit. He had to know if Mom was all right.

The weather was cold and damp but he continued to pant. He cocked his ears, listening for the slightest indication of activity. He pressed his twitching nose against the laundry room window and whispered.

"Feathers, Feathers, are you there? Sweetheart, are you okay? Oh, please be all right, Feathers, please be all right," he pleaded.

Again he noticed the movement. He was sure of it this time. Within seconds a pointed little nose poked its way out of the pile of rubble. It was Bean. She was covered with sweat. Her eyes were deep in her small face and she looked as though she had not slept in hours. And, of course, she hadn't.

"Bean, Bean, I'm so happy to see you. What's going on? Where is my Feathers? I can hardly breathe. I don't think I can take much more of this," Beaux ranted. "What's going on?"

Quieting Dad down, Bean explained.

"Hush up, Beaux. She's doing the best she can. You know this hasn't been an easy time for Feathers. She's through the worst of it, though. The last few hours have been really hectic. She was very anxious and frightened. I couldn't leave her for a moment to let you know she was in labor. But I think just hearing your voice has settled her down. We'll just have to let her instincts take over now. I think she's about ready to deliver. You just stay put. I've got to get back. And, oh, by the way, she said she loves you."

Bean quickly returned to the tunnel she had forged for herself, and within minutes Dad could detect a flurry of activity in Mom's nesting place.

He only had to wait a short while (which to Dad it seemed like hours) before he heard cries and whimpers. He saw papers and dirty clothes being pushed and tossed. But he still couldn't see his Feathers.

Mom was totally occupied at the moment. She had known the night before that she was almost ready to deliver, but she was so anxious and nervous she didn't know what to do first. At about 1 a.m. she shifted into automatic pilot and began to gather old papers and dirty clothes. Bean stopped by after a night at the local convenience store trashcans and was at first confused.

"Feathers, what are you doing up so late? It's after midnight. Quite a bit after midnight, actually. You need your rest."

"I don't know, Bean. I just have this need to get things in order. I feel like I need a safe, dark, quiet shelter."

Bean immediately went to work.

"Okay Feathers, I guess this is it."

The two of them pushed and stacked and crumbled until a small nesting area was prepared.

After several hours of restless tossing and turning, the minute Mom heard Dad's soft whispers coming through the window, she finally began to breathe smoothly and evenly. A wonderful calm came over her when she sensed his strong presence outside her room, her anxiety and fear dissolved. She began to relax, and dispatched Bean to reassure Dad that all was well.

By the time Bean returned to the fabricated nest, Mom was gently licking the smallest little bundle of goo that Bean had ever seen. I was now officially part of the world.

"Oh, my gosh," Bean exclaimed. "What have you done without me? What is that? It looks awful."

She scurried up next to Mom, crinkling up her nose, and peeked over at a four-ounce pile of slime. Barely glancing up at Bean, Mom slowly but surely licked and licked, cleaning and preening me until tufts of soft feather-like fuzz began to appear.

"Oh Bean, she is so beautiful. She's like a small golden peach. She is so fuzzy. Go ahead, feel how soft. Oh, she's just a little ball of love."

Mom couldn't see my deep brown eyes, yet. Eyes just like my Dad's. But, by feeling the shape of my small body while cleaning me with her gentle tongue, she could tell that I was going to have many of her and Dad's characteristics.

"Oh Bean, I can feel her beautiful little legs. She has delicate Pekinese legs. And her nose, it's so sharp and straight, just like Beaux's."

As for Bean, all she could say was, "Whatever. It looks awfully wet to me. I guess I'd better go give Beaux the news. Are you sure it's a girl? How can you tell? It's so little."

Never missing a beat or taking her eyes off of me for one second, Mom just smiled.

"Trust me, Bean, a Mother can tell."

Bean gave Dad the news. He swooned and pranced and

howled, alerting the entire animal neighborhood. All day long he sent birth announcements via howls and barks. Congratulations came back in all forms. Two local squirrels gathered nuts and branch twigs, leaving them near Dad's cushion as their tribute to his new pup. A nest of long-legged spiders spun a beautiful web intertwined with small blue flecks of fly wings across the top of the laundry room window. Needles, Willie, and Bean were not to be outdone. The three of them spent several hours at the local hamburger joint pillaging small bits of meat to bring back to Mom for her and her baby.

When BJ returned from work and came to the backyard to check on all the noise, it was as though she, too, understood what had happened. She firmly rubbed Dad's ears.

"Good man, Beaux. Good man."

He was so proud. If only he could hold Feathers and his little girl. But for now he would have to be content to admire them both from his window roost.

The Granites were gone most of the time, finalizing their plans to move away. When they were at the house, they came separately. Mr. Granite planned his visits to arrive when Mrs. Granite was at work. He would sneak in the back door and rummage through drawers and closets, looking for things to hide, like a squirrel storing nuts for the winter. It never occurred to him to check on Mom.

Although Mrs. Granite was still living at the house, she spent many evenings away. When she did come home, she would just throw her dirty clothes into the laundry room, sometimes with a partially eaten sandwich or a dried out hamburger. She never bothered, either, to see if Mom was all right.

I can hardly remember the first few weeks. I know that I was tired and hungry. But, Mom took care of everything. She never left my side, and my love for her grew deeper by the minute. When I was about twelve days old, I could see her face. It was then that I realized she was the most beautiful dog in the world. Just being held next to her tummy was heaven.

My life was like a fairy tale. Mom caressed me, cleaned me, fed me, and held me. Dad was at the window almost constantly, peering in to check on us. Urging Mom to make sure I was warm, checking to make sure I wasn't hungry. He dispatched Needles, Willie, and Bean to get the scraps of food he had saved for us. He was the best Dad in the world. He accepted responsibility for our family and immediately took charge.

I could hardly help but ham it up. They were such a hungry audience. My every move thrilled them. The first time I opened my eyes, Mom swooned so loud and long I thought she would need oxygen.

"Oh Beaux, oh Bean, just look at those eyes. She's got her father's eyes. Oh, no they're deeper brown than Beaux's eyes. They are even more beautiful than your eyes, Beaux," she exclaimed. "Can you see? Quick. Get closer to the window. I'll try and slide her over in the light. Hurry, take a look."

It was wonderful.

Needles and Willie just shrugged their shoulders in despair, teasing Mom and Dad the way good friends do. Willie was just happy that Mom couldn't finish all the bits of food Needles and Bean brought in. He lay around in the dirty clothes, snacking and observing all the ogling.

One of my very fondest memories was the time I actually stood up on all four legs—at once. At first I could only manage to stand up on my two back legs, pushing my face and chest into the floor. When I managed to stand on my front legs, I was forced to sit down. I just couldn't seem to do all four together.

One afternoon, while Mom was taking a nap and Dad had gone to do his hourly watch, I was lying against Mom's tummy. While she was sleeping, I decided I'd try and stretch a little. I rolled away from her soft belly, kind of like a ball does. It was so much fun. I loved to roll around, especially when Mom pushed me with her nose. After about three or four rotations I ended up on my back with all four of my fuzzy paws shooting straight up in the air. I was still shaped so much like a little ball that, scramble as I might, I was just not able to turn over.

Uncle Needles, arriving in the nick of time, suggested a remedy.

"Hey, kiddo, what's up? Whatcha doing on your back like that? You look like a small peach with four furry twigs. Ya know, you look kinda silly."

"Oh, Uncle Needles," I said quietly, not wanting to disturb Mom, "I really don't know how I got into this position. I was only trying to stretch my legs and somehow I ended up upside-down."

"Yeah, well them things happen, kid. But, let's see what we're gonna do now."

Walking all around me, Uncle Needles surveyed the situation. He poked his tail and his nose underneath my ball-like body. He walked to one end of the room, counting to himself, and then to the other.

"Okay, kiddo, I got an idea. You just lay there and count the stars. Keep breathing nice and easy, and then when I count to THREE: One, Two, Three. Just like that, then, you get ready for the ride of your life. Got it? One, Two Three."

I did just like Uncle Needles said. I just lay there and looked up at the ceiling, except I couldn't find any stars.

Uncle Needles scurried to a corner of the room and started to make a funny noise, like the humming of the dryer. He sounded so silly, I couldn't help but smile and laugh. I couldn't see him, but his little sounds were getting louder and louder. All of a sudden, he squeaked out a sharp, "One, Two, Three."

It was just after the three that I felt a tiny, but mighty poke, right under my back. It was so quick it slid me first in a circle and then in a roll. I was sailing around the floor. All of a sudden, swoosh, into the air I went. After about three airborne somersaults I was standing on all four feet.

I was very weak and I didn't think I could stay that way for very long. On all four at once, that is. But, Uncle Needles helped steady me by sliding a puffy piece of crumbled up newspaper under my tummy. After a few minutes I was able to stand up long enough to take one step and then two, and finally three. When I fell flat on my backside I heard cheers from Mom who had been quietly watching from her nap area, and from Dad who had returned to his window. They were so proud. Uncle Needles couldn't stop boasting about helping me take my very first steps.

CHAPTER 19

🐾

Opened Eyes Bring Tear Drops

The humans call it Halloween. I quickly learned it was a day people played bad tricks on each other. I was twenty-nine days old. Our schedule had changed dramatically. I hardly ever got to roll around anymore, and we no longer had the washer and dryer to hide behind. As I lay by Mom's tummy and heart I could tell by the tenseness of her body that something was amiss. My instinct for danger had already developed and I sensed I was no longer safe. Mom tried to soothe and reassure me, but I knew we were in danger.

Over the last few days there was a lot of new activity at the house. The Granites still didn't spend too much time there, but realtors and repairmen were in and around constantly. Dad was able to come by only occasionally and then for short visits. It seemed like time stood still, yet the days passed very quickly.

Mom tried to prepare me for the changes ahead, but no one could predict what was in store for us. The memory of her words still causes my ears to shoot straight back on my head and my nose to quiver!

Oftentimes after I had left her, when I was very scared and very lonely, I would just roll up like a little ball, like I used to when I rested near her tummy and her heart, and I would dream about the few weeks we had together. That's how we spent our last hours with each other, me lying next to her tummy and heart, and she just licking my head and ears, talking softly to me, telling me how much she loved me.

"Sweetheart, my little sunshine girl," Mom said, "I have something very important to tell you. Mr. and Mrs. Granite are going to have to leave the house for good today and I am afraid that when they find us together they are going to do something very bad. I don't know what it will be, but I think we have to be prepared for the very worst. They may throw us away in a plastic bag, or try to drown us, or just leave us here, locked up in this house. Those things would be very bad, but I would gladly accept them if I had to. What I fear most is them taking you away from me. I don't know how I would cope with that. Whatever happens, I know will happen very fast and so I must remind you of all the things I have been trying to teach you over the last few weeks."

Mom started to remind me about all sorts of things that little dogs and puppies, and even little children should do to be safe, but I couldn't hear any of it. All I could think of was the unthinkable. Being away from my Mom. My eyes had only been opened for a short time, but tears were already beginning to fall from them.

The last boxes of household goods and pieces of furniture had been taken away earlier in the morning. The house was empty and the Granites were making a final walk through. They hadn't been in the laundry room for days, having left the last cleanup to some hired workers. Their voices grew louder as they approached our room. Mom and I just clung to each other. We no longer had any place to hide. The washer and dryer were gone, along with all the dirty clothes, crumbled up newspapers and packing supplies. The cleaning people had removed everything. All that was left was a small makeshift container of water, and me and Mom.

The Granites were arguing as usual.

"Gladys, you agreed to it. I specifically heard you say I could have the salt and pepper shakers." It was Mr. Granite's voice. "And now, after everything is packed, you decide you want them back. Gladys, this is just one more of your tactics to drive me crazy."

Mrs. Granite blurted out, "Well, George, you have to admit, it won't be a very long trip. You have been well on your way to gaga land for a long time."

Their voices carried through the empty house, echoing off the bare walls and floors.

No matter what the breed, breaking up a family causes stress, and in this case the Granites were not unique. His thinning hair usually spread smoothly and meticulously across his bony scalp, looked like a Wire Terriers, split and frizzled. His nose showed thin red lines spreading down into the upper parts of his cheeks, like red spider legs crawling out of his bloodshot eyes. He smelled hard and sharp, like the fumes from the back of the car or the garage floor.

Like a dog that pathetically attends one competition too many,

Mrs. Granite took great pains to prepare herself for the day. At first glance, she looked somewhat improved. Prancing like the pick of the litter, she preened and purred, but her empty eyes told a different story. She seemed almost pre-rabid!

Mom and I were not in much better shape. With no old dirty clothes or crumbled newspapers or ripped up rags to lie on, the laundry room was cold and damp. The electricity had been shut off earlier in the day and the approaching night sky cast a dark shadow across the floor. I had never known the cold before. The whiskers at the end of my nose started to tremble and the sensation continued across my back, into my stomach and down my legs. I could not control the spasms in my body and the blinking of my eyes.

Mom did her best to soothe me, but her own trembling body betrayed her efforts. She was shaking uncontrollably. Over and over she looked to the window, hoping to see Dad, needing his guidance and strength more than ever.

"Oh Beaux, oh darling Beaux, where are you? We need you so very much. Where are you?"

It wasn't until later that night Mom would learn that the hired workers had reinforced the broken fence slats, and removed all of the piled up debris, preventing any further visits from Dad. Even Needles, Willie, and Bean were having a difficult time getting in to see Mom and me. The house was so empty there was no defense against detection.

We were alone. We had no one but each other, and even that would end soon.

CHAPTER 20

Our Life Together Comes to an End

Should I live for one hundred dog years, I will never forget the sound the laundry room door made that late afternoon. It was the loudest cracking boom I've ever heard. Like an explosion blowing up my world.

CRACK! BOOM! Mr. Granite slammed the laundry room door into its pocket with such force it shook the house and slid back into a closed position. The first slam of the door was in response to his frustration with Mrs. Granite, who continued to nag at him while she followed from room to room. The second

time he slammed the door, it was in response to seeing Mom and me huddled in the corner, a bundle of whimpers and shivers.

"What is this, Gladys? I thought you took care of that mutt of yours, and where did that little runty thing come from?"

Looking befuddled, Mrs. Granite stammered, "Well, well, uh, I don't know, uh, I haven't seen Feathers for so long I thought she ran away. I am sure I told one of the workers to get rid of her. This room has been such a mess, and uh, I was busy too, George, so don't lay this on me."

Almost immediately, upon hearing his description of me, Mom jumped to her feet, and, shielding me from his view, began to bark and snap at Mr. Granite.

We were so weakened from our fear and terror I will never know how Mom summoned up the strength to growl at Mr. Granite, but growl she did.

When Mrs. Granite approached, Mom did the same thing. Turning from one and then to the other, she courageously tried to protect me from their grip. But, of course, it was a losing battle from the start. Frantically scurrying around the room, Mom's barks and pleas bounced throughout the vacant house.

Mr. Granite was shaking. His anger was so intense the room began to heat up. He looked at Mrs. Granite with such disgust she practically shrunk into the corner. It was hard to distinguish her whimpers from my own.

Mom, trying her best to protect me, finally looked pleadingly to her masters, as if to say, "What more do you want from me? What more can I give you? I'm begging you with all my heart. Please just leave us alone."

Struck with just a brief moment of compassion, or maybe just laziness, Mrs. Granite spoke. "George, let's just leave them. No one will find them until we're gone, and then who will care?"

Still seething, unable to control the frustration of his years of confinement with this old biddie, he turned toward Mrs. Granite with a look of total revulsion.

"That is *exactly* what you would like, isn't it Gladys? Just one more set up. Just like all these years of ambushes and backstabbing. Leave them here. And then, when their dried up pathetic bodies are discovered, and we get arrested for cruelty to animals, you will say, 'Oh, but Judge, I begged him not to do it. But, he threatened me. I love animals.' Oh, no Gladys, not this time. Never again."

All at once, Mr. Granite drew his foot back, and with the force of an angry mule, struck Mom so hard her body hit the back wall and slid to the floor like a bag of damp leaves. I was frozen. I was sure she was dead.

"Now, clean that thing up and I'll get rid of this one on my way out of town."

I was immediately scooped up and shoved into the side pocket of Mr. Granite's jacket.

Mrs. Granite went up to Mom's body. Scanning the room she saw a partially used roll of paper towels still in the wall dispenser. She pulled the remaining sheets off the roll, and wrapped Mom up as though she were a piece of spoiled meat. Walking out of her house for the last time, she stopped at the edge of the kitchen, picked up her purse, and slammed the door. She dropped Mom's body into a discarded packing box at the end of the property.

Mice have very sharp senses, and as soon as Willie heard someone approaching the cardboard container, he immediately tunneled deep into the contents of the old box. The thud was a surprise, but also the hope of some new treat. This particular refuse, however, did not hold any pleasure for Willie.

Until now, Willie was having a field day rummaging through the fast food containers the movers threw out. He would have settled for an old piece of cheese or some dried noodles, or just about anything that a young mouse could eat. But, no such luck. So far all he found was a bunch of soiled rags and old ripped up sheets and towels. That is, until he heard the thud.

When he finally burrowed back to the top of the heap he encountered Mom's small mangled body. He immediately came to her aid. He began to gnaw away at the paper toweling surrounding her face. He was in a dither.

"Feathers, oh my, Feathers, whatever happened to you? Oh no, don't talk. Just rest. You can tell us later. Just try to breathe evenly. Let me get this paper out of the way, and then I'll go for help."

Gnawing and spitting out the bits of toweling, Willie moved as fast as he could. Finally, making sure the paper did not hinder her breathing, Willie took a good look at Mom's face. He was horrified. Her pain and despair were indescribable. It was only then that he realized Mom was alone. Gasping, he wondered *where was her baby?*

Mom could not speak, but only stared at Willie with pleading eyes. When he was sure he could do no more alone, he told Mom he was on his way for help.

"Feathers, just hold on. I'm on my way for help. You should be safe here until I get back. Just hold on. Please hold on!"

Willie jumped from the trash bin and scurried to Dad's backyard. My life with Mom had come to an end.

CHAPTER 21

Beaux's Second Chance at Mr. Granite

Outside in the driveway things were not as quiet. Waiting for Mrs. Granite to move her car so he could be on his way, Mr. Granite propped his foot up on his fender and reached into his jacket for a cigarette. It was only then that he realized I was in his oversized pocket. Without a second glance, he tossed me into the opened window and onto the floor.

I really couldn't think of anything to do. Actually, I couldn't think at all. My shock at seeing my Mom kicked into the wall and then me being stuffed into a musty old jacket made my senses stop. I could see the floor of the car, but I had no idea what it was. I could smell the soiled rubber mats, but it registered nothing in my mind. I was numb.

Mr. Granite fumbled with his pack of cigarettes as Mrs. Granite approached, got into her car, and began to back out of the driveway. No one noticed Willie, accompanied by a highly agitated Needles and Bean, talking to Dad.

Mr. Granite, edging up to Mrs. Granite's car, spoke into her opened window.

"Well, Gladys, I hope you were able to take care of that one, small, minute detail without too much difficulty. I know these things are hard for you, but…"

Before he could finish his sentence, he noticed Mrs. Granite's eyes focused on something behind him. As he turned to look he heard a deep, gut-wrenching snarl.

It was Dad. His fury building, he stood rigidly on the driveway, poised for an attack. As though seeing Dad on a different level for the first time, Mr. Granite instinctively knew that he had crossed a boundary in Dad's world and that he would not be contained.

After leaving Mom, Willie found the mice and Dad anxiously waiting for the Granites to leave their house one last time. Everyone was on edge, but Willie's report of Mom's fate put fire in Dad's eyes. Dad went into a zone even Needles had never before seen. Mr. Granite had attempted to destroy Dad's family. He would have to pay.

By rote, Dad dispatched Needles and Bean to attend to Mom. He ordered Willie to gather other friends and begin a search for me. He had to know if I was dead or alive. Finally, and best of all, he would have another chance at Mr. Granite.

Dad leaped into the air with the agility of a Siamese cat. Clearing the gate bordering the driveway, he aimed for Mr. Granite's neck. He was going for his jugular.

Alerted by Dad's snarl, Mr. Granite managed to turn his body toward Dad and raise his arm above his face. Dad was only able to grip Mr. Granite's lower arm. He tore into his jacket and flesh, ripping away at both. Mrs. Granite quickly rolled up her window and began to sound her horn. Dad backed away from the car and slowly began to circle Mr. Granite. He did not want to rush this. He was going to take his time. Mr. Granite was frozen in place. He face was ashen. Blood was coming from his arm and he had several deep scratches below his eye. Never taking his terrified gaze off of Dad, he screamed above the blaring horn for Mrs. Granite to do something.

"*GLADYS*, do something. Run over the beast. Call the police. Do something!"

Mrs. Granite slowly backed her rusted Honda out of the driveway. Her horn no longer blasting, she rolled down her window and yelled, "You handle it, George. I know these things are hard for you, but..." her voice trailing off until she and her drab gray jalopy were out of sight.

Dad continued to circle while Mr. Granite attempted to edge his way toward his car. In response to all the outside commotion, BJ opened her front door only to find Dad stalking a terror-stricken Mr. Granite. Running down the driveway with Dad's leash in hand, BJ was horrified to think what must have happened to bring Dad to such a state. She was confident that his anger was justified. Nevertheless, she knew she would have to stop him, for his own good.

Approaching Dad from behind, she spoke very softly, but firmly.

"Beaux, Beaux. I want you to back off now. Back off, Beaux."

Dad stood his ground, his concentration total. He was very

conflicted, but he had already made up his mind his life would be worth nothing without Mom and me. He was willing to sacrifice himself in our defense. It was his job. He was our protector.

"Beaux, I know that what you're doing seems right to you now, but please back off."

With BJ taking charge of the situation, Mr. Granite began to gain confidence, and so to let his mouth run off, as well.

"You'd just better get this animal away from me. Do you hear me? I'm going to sue you for everything you've got. I'll see to it that this mongrel ends up the same way as Feathers and her mutt."

Dad could take no more. Again he lunged at Mr. Granite, hitting him with such force he was propelled into the bumper of his car. A spray of blood shot out of a deep gash in the back of his head, then trickled down over his shirt collar. Stunned, Mr. Granite groveled and turned himself over, ending up on all fours, face to face with Dad.

Dad approached him. He was in total control. He knew it, and so did Mr. Granite. He circled Mr. Granite, a deep growl emanating from his soul. He was aware of BJ behind him, slowly approaching with his leash, but he was not to be deterred. He lowered his head, narrowed his eyes, and bared his sharp teeth. The muscles in his shoulders and front paws became taut and stretched; he moved with deliberate cunning, circling his prey.

Mr. Granite was speechless. Still on all fours, his limbs trembled. His face was all at once ashen, blood splattered and drenched in sweat. He was now at Dad's mercy.

Almost touching Mr. Granite's face with his own, Dad looked deep into his eyes and instinctively knew that he, a dog, was the more humane, better male. Realizing this, he gave one more deep growl and backed off. BJ, understanding, softly stroked his strong head and said, "Good man, Beaux, good man." (And he was.)

Mr. Granite was still disoriented, but managed to stagger to his feet.

"All right, Mr. Granite, I guess we know who the better man is. Now, I suggest you leave this place and never return. For your sake, that is."

"Okay, Okay. Just get hold of that beast and keep him down until I get into my car. I don't want any more trouble, either. I just want outta here."

BJ proudly took hold of Dad until Mr. Granite was safely in his car. He closed all of his windows, and began to back out of the driveway. When the car turned so the passenger side was visible to Dad and BJ, they saw a small, fuzzy, distressed little puppy, pawing at the side window. Dad attempted to lunge at the car, but for that one fateful split-second his heart stopped and he lost all of his strength. Part of him had died and his own weakness prevented him from pursuing Mr. Granite any further.

CHAPTER 22

Granite, the Hardest Stone of All

BJ began to run toward the Granites' back yard, hoping to find Mom abandoned in the laundry room, ready to be rescued by her and Dad. What she found, however, was quite a different scene. Even BJ was unprepared for the last callous act of the Granites.

Dad ran straight to the crumbled container in which Mom had been tossed. BJ, immediately behind him, stopped to see what fascination the old box held. Hearing whines, BJ slowly approached.

Needles, Willie, and Bean immediately scurried out of sight, but not before passing their good wishes along to Dad. He gave his signal back and they knew they'd, again, done a good job.

At first glance, BJ thought Dad was intrigued by a discarded, soiled dust mop. All she could see was a twisted, oily looking clump of tattered rags. When she looked closer her gasp betrayed her surprise.

Her stomach began to rise in her mouth and she felt she would heave uncontrollably. Mom, hardly breathing, was laying on a pile of old sheets and ripped towels. Torn paper toweling was stuck to her face and eyes. There was an open wound on her side, and dried, crusted blood coated her hair. The heavy odor of cleaning fluids permeated the cardboard. Mom appeared to be alive, but just barely.

Standing over the box, peering in at Mom, Dad's tears softly fell on her face. BJ gently lifted Mom from her intended grave. While her physical agony was obvious, only Mom could know the pain of losing her puppy. Even her love for Dad was, at this moment, of no consolation. There was no way to measure the pain of losing a child, and no source of comfort existed to heal the wound. In her mind, her world ended the moment her puppy was torn from her arms.

She could find no strength to aid her labored breathing. If it had not been for Dad and BJ's intervention, Mom would have quietly died, as intended.

At the sight of Mom, discarded in the trash bin like a piece of rotten meat, BJ felt immediate regret in having helped Mr. Granite escape. She shuddered to think of what Dad would have done had she not interceded in Mr. Granite's behalf. Yet, she was so sorry she did. Glancing at Beaux, BJ knew she would have to wait in line if Mr. Granite ever dared to return to the neighborhood.

Mom needed tending to, and immediately. Calmly talking to Dad and reassuring him, BJ walked slowly to the house with Mom safely cradled in her arms, all the time praying that her injuries would not prove fatal.

Mom glanced at Dad through the paper towel bits. She knew

CousCous Mackey

his despair was as deep as her own, but she had no energy to give to him for his pain.

In spite of his deep love for Mom, Dad's grieving required all the strength he had for himself. They would each need their own time and their own space to recover from this loss. It was not an agony they could share.

CHAPTER 23

Trick or Treat

As we drove away from the house I could still hear my Dad's guttural howl. I knew he could not hear me because my wailing was inside. I was much too frightened to cause a fuss, and it took all my strength just to prop myself up against the window to get one last look at my home. I would not allow myself to think of my Mom.

I could still hear the sound of Mr. Granite's foot hitting her side and then her whimpering sighs before she slammed into the wall. I was very confused. I didn't understand any of it. I had never witnessed such cruel acts. They all seemed so unnecessary to me. Mr. and Mrs. Granite had so many other options, but they chose the ones that would hurt us the most. It just made no sense.

The car had a bitter cigarette odor that settled on my tongue and burned my eyes. It was full of Mr. Granite's last-minute moving efforts. Moldy socks, unwashed shirts, rancid shoes. I fought as hard as I could to pull myself out of my shocked state and try to think of what I might do to save myself. But, my terror was too great to come up with a plan. I just burrowed myself back into Mr. Granite's jacket pocket, and helplessly waited for the events to unfold.

Mr. Granite was beginning to recover from his humiliating encounter. When he massaged the back of his neck he felt a sticky substance cover his fingers. He brought his hand to his face and a wave of sweetness entered his nostrils. Looking down and seeing his blood-covered hand, Mr. Granite's shock turned into fear, and then, anger.

He drove so fast the car was swerving in and out of the paths of approaching traffic. He called the other driver's stupid jerks, and worse. He kept cursing Mrs. Granite, BJ, and my Mom and Dad. He slammed the steering wheel with his hand and then swore in pain.

I don't know for how long we drove, but it seemed like forever. We turned in one direction and then another. We stopped and waited, and then started up again. At one point we slowed up and then with a flash started to go very fast. I could hear lots of other cars around us and horns blowing as Mr. Granite moved the car from side to side.

He began to mumble to himself, making a verbal list of the things he needed to do. "Get to the hospital. Yeah, I better do that. That damn mongrel might have rabies. Get some gas, just about out of gas. Pick up some beer before I go home. Yeh, need some brewskis."

And on and on he went.

After a while, Mr. Granite began to search his pockets, throwing bits of paper and partially used matches in the air.

"Now where are those damn cigarettes? I know I have them here somewhere," he said irritably.

Finding none in his shirt and trouser pockets, he started to rummage through the discarded clothes and bags and even the old shoes strewn around the floor and seats of the car.

He steered with one hand and threw his arm and shoulder over the seatback trying to grab at old clothes in the back seat. His frustration was starting to mount again. The next thing I felt was a sharp turn. Mr. Granite yelled, "If you can't drive on the freeway, keep off!" Finally the car skidded to a stop.

The door opened and slammed and Mr. Granite got out. We had pulled into a big opened lot where people were going in and out of a building, carrying bags and bottles. Later, I learned it was called a convenience store.

I couldn't see any way out of my mess. The doors and windows were closed and I had no idea what I would do if I were able to escape. I'd never been away from Mom. And I had never been so scared. I just continued to huddle in the old jacket, waiting for my fate to happen.

When Mr. Granite came back to the car he started to back out of the driveway, while rummaging through his pockets. "Now where is that blasted lighter? I know I have it here somewhere. I distinctly remember putting it in my jacket."

His voice was loud and his breathing was erratic, just like it was in the laundry room when he hurt my Mom. I closed my eyes and began to shake. I was not cold in the car, but my teeth began to chatter and my bones stiffened up, making my body feel like a vibrating board.

"That's it. My jacket. That's where that blasted lighter is. Now where is that stupid thing?"

Turning his head to the side, looking right into the passenger seat, he found his jacket. As he pulled at it, searching for his lighter, I rolled out of the pocket and onto the floor. The next few minutes were a blur to me.

Mr. Granite's first look was one of surprise. He had completely forgotten about me. Then, within a few seconds his look turned to anger, but very quickly turned to a sneer. The car screeched to a stop one more time. Mr. Granite leaned over to the right and grabbed me by my neck. He pulled me up so fast and with such force my breathing stopped for a moment. He put his face to mine and, almost hissing at me, said, "Well, little runt, trick or treat."

The door opened and I was flung into the path of an oncoming car. Without a second look, he drove away.

There was a loud screeching sound and the car came to an abrupt halt. Next a bunch of rowdy Halloween beggars, anxious to play bad jokes, jumped out of the car and ran into the entrance of the store shouting, "Trick or treat!"

I hoped their surprise would be better than mine.

CHAPTER 24

Taking One Day at a Time

After BJ had safely carried Mom into the house, she immediately called an emergency clinic and followed instructions to check Mom for internal injuries. "Okay now, sweetheart. Let's just check to see if it's okay to move you to the doctor."

"Let's see that little paw; can we move it okay?" She gingerly moved Mom's paws and felt her tummy and rubbed all over her bruised body. She carefully washed the blood from Mom's face and side and sprayed a liquid antibiotic over the wounds. It was important for Mom to take in some moisture, but it would not have been prudent for her to swallow large amounts of liquid. BJ carefully placed a few drops of water on Mom's tongue.

Convinced it was safe to take her in the car, she prepared for the drive to Dad's regular veterinarian. She loosely wrapped Mom in a clean, dry, white towel, hoping it would keep her safe and warm until she could get professional care. Dad was always close behind.

As BJ gathered her wallet and keys, Dad stood over the sofa cushion and gently licked Mom's forehead to further clean the patches of silky hair that framed her delicate face. All he could say was, "One day at a time. We just have to take it one day at a time."

Mom could not respond. She was inconsolable. Her heart had been broken for the second time. Her chest felt like it held shards of glass. Using all the strength she could muster she slowly curled up into the fetal position. She could not imagine ever straightening her body again. Dad softly laid his jaw on the cushion next to her anguished face. When BJ returned to the room Dad instinctively became alert. Then, remembering that they were in a safe place, he sunk to the floor and let out a deep sigh.

Carefully lifting Mom in her arms, BJ turned to Dad.

"Yes, my dear Beaux, you must come, too."

As they backed out of the driveway, BJ took one more glance at the Granite home. It was as though an aura of evil surrounded it.

In the vet's able care, Mom was cleaned, stitched and x-rayed. Her broken ribs required secure bandaging, and her bruised lung would need lots of rest and quiet. Her injured soul was another story. Not surprisingly, her broken bones and battered body would heal long before her heart.

A lifetime seemed to have passed by the time the three of them returned home. Mom was placed on a large, soft pillow, as Dad obediently stood guard. Before BJ left the room, she rubbed his head, and then gently placed her lips on Mom's forehead, "We'll all get through this, I promise you," she said. "We will just have to take it one day at a time."

Dad watched as Mom drifted into a restless sleep.

CHAPTER 25

🐾

Seven-Eleven—My Lucky Number

The parking lot was a whirl of tiny dust particles and bits and pieces of fast food paper wrappers. My eyes frantically searched for a safe haven out of the wind, but the October air was already frigid and it caused me to tear up and blink. I couldn't focus. Wheels screeched. Doors slammed. I could sense cars everywhere. Drivers yelled at their passengers, and at each other. I was overwhelmed.

Relying on my whiskers and hearing, I scurried to one side of the lot hoping to avoid getting flattened by the flurry of traffic. The trick or treaters, having been rebuked by the convenience store owner, began to leave in an angry mood. They were loaded with energy and looking for someone, or something, to release it on. By the time they saw me I had no place to hide.

The group leader, dressed all in black with white grease paint covering his entire face, noticed me first. "Hey, guys, look here. I got me a real Halloween treat. This is something we can *definitely* have some fun with."

He yanked me up by my neck and shook me from side to side. My body rolled up and back and I felt as though my head was no longer attached to my spine. He tossed me into the arms of one of his buddies.

This one was dressed in a dark-colored body suit, with a tail sewn into his backside. A makeshift cape covered his shoulders and back, and two horns were interwoven in his long, stringy hair. I remembered a story my Mother told me about good and evil, and what evil looked like in the form of a human. This guy had the same look.

He groped at me as though I were a pile of matted rubbish. After he thoroughly studied me, he said, "Hey, guys, do you think this little mutt will land on its feet, like a cat does, you know? If we throw it up in the air?"

Looking to answer his own question, he yanked at my tail, and began to twirl me in a large circle.

The last one, the meanest one of all, grabbed me in mid-twirl. He started to shove me into a rough feeling bag that smelled of gasoline. I couldn't see his face because he wore a heavy rubber mask. I could only smell his sour breath.

"Let's give that jerk inside the store a real treat—we'll light up his life, and his night. The cheap creep."

He just about had me in the bag when he asked one of his partners for a match.

Several of the store customers gathered around to watch the festivities. Only one had the courage to try and save my life.

Smaller in stature than the trick-or-treaters, but far bigger in courage and compassion, he walked up to the rubber-faced jokester, and looking him square in his eyes, said, "Whatcha got there, buddy? Looks to me like that puppy is gonna be in for a pretty bad time. Why don't you just give me the little dog and go on your way."

The boy with the rubber face was no different than any other bully. As long as he had his groupies around him he was brave. He looked at his buddies and said, "Hey, guys, we've got a hero here. Let's see if we have any tricks for him."

Several of the other customers began to take an interest and the momentum was about to change. Sensing this, it took but a few seconds for Rubber Face's buddies to scramble to their car and leave their partner, literally holding the bag, with me in it.

No longer backed up by his two goons, Rubber Face couldn't scramble away fast enough.

"Hey man, I don't want no trouble. You want this little mutt? Hey, cool. It's okay with me, man. Just take the bag, it don't belong to me."

Tossing the bag, and its contents, toward the customer he turned tail and ran down the street. Once again, I was at the mercy of a stranger.

Neither in nor out of the bag the jostling and all the events of the day made me sick to my stomach and scared to death. This last harrowing experience almost finished me off. I was a mess.

My new stranger gently pulled me from the bag and ruffled my fur with sure hands. He lifted me to his face, and smelled my coat.

"Well, maybe it can be a happy Halloween, after all. Gasoline doesn't seem to have gotten into your skin. Nice bath and a good brush—you'll be good as new."

Then he let out a laugh like nothing I ever heard before. It was like a roar. A roar I would look forward to hearing and that would lift my spirits for many weeks to come.

I had no concept of time, but I knew it was late. And, I knew I was hungry, and thirsty, too. My new friend must have known it as well. Firmly holding me in his arms, he walked back into the store and ordered two hot dogs and a Coke.

My, he had a booming voice! "Hey, buddy. How about a couple of dogs for me and my little gal here? And you'd better add a Coke, she's got to be thirsty, too." And then, the laugh.

The proprietor was delighted to oblige. "My pleasure, friend. My pleasure, indeed. And, it's on the house. It's the least I can do!"

What a laugh that got.

His short-cropped hair was streaked with silver and wisps of it fell on his forehead. Like Mr. Granite he had on a jacket, but this one smelled of rich scents, like *fresh* coffee, and sweet donuts. It was soft and comforting when he held me against it.

We took our hot dogs and Coke out to the parking lot where we sat on the pavement. I cuddled as close as I could get. He broke off a small piece of the steaming meat and placed it in the flat of his hand. Offering it, he said, "Well, darlin', you'd better eat up. I can't take this food home 'cause Sasha and all her friends will want a piece. We'd better finish it off right here and now. We'll decide what we're gonna do with you a little later."

Mom taught me not to accept food from strangers. But, I hadn't eaten for so long, and fearing I might not get another chance for a long while, I gobbled up the hot dog as quickly as I could. Over time, I learned that I should not have worried. This man was very kind, and before I knew it, there was yet another piece of hot dog placed at my nose.

I was nestled in the passenger seat of a small, dark car. It was warm inside and smelled of more hot dogs, mustard, French fries and coffee, all the things the moving people shared with Mom and me. It also had the scent of another dog and a myriad of other animals, too. It wouldn't be long before I would meet them all.

With my tummy full, I started to feel warm and not so afraid. But, thoughts of Mom and Dad crept into my mind. I couldn't bear to think about the events of the last few hours. I didn't know where I was or where I was going. I didn't know how far away from my home I had been taken or where my new home would be. I didn't know if my Mom was dead or alive. All I did know was that I was terribly tired and terribly sad.

CHAPTER 26

Green Shutters and a Snowflake

Home was a sight to behold. We pulled up to the house with a screech of the wheels. I rolled onto the front floorboard that was covered with a large crumpled towel, which felt very much like the texture of my Mom's soft hair. I didn't want to get off it, and just nuzzled my nose into its nap. The car door opened and I was swooped up in the towel, and then, almost immediately placed onto the lawn. My rescuer scratched my ears and neck and then happily pronounced, "Well, little girl, this is your new home."

The house was made of white wood and most of the windows had green wooden shutters around them. Some of the windows had green shutters lying beneath them. In the large window facing the street, a big, carved-out pumpkin sat with a glowing face. On the front porch, right beneath the light, a big bag of wrapped candies sat, with a sign saying, *"One per customer please! Have a safe Halloween!"*

It wasn't a big house, like BJ's, but it sat in the middle of a large lot with many trees and bushes on it. The lawn was cut, but because it was late fall there were piles of blowing leaves and tree branches covering the brown grass. The garage stood alone, away from the house, and seemed to be tilted to one side. It looked as though the next good wind might take it down.

"Now listen, little girl. You'd better take care of your business before we go in, 'cause I'll be goin' out in a little while and I don't think you're big enough to make it through the doggie door."

I got another rub on the neck and a scratching of the ears.

Before tonight my life had been confined to the laundry room of the Granites' home, and although Mom had taught me many things, I had only been exposed to a limited number of smells. But now, as I walked around the front yard, I started to become aware of all sorts of odors and scents. I could tell lots of animals had been on this lawn before me. And my dog sense told me that many of them were close by.

We approached the front of the house. I stood ready to enter, when the key went into the lock and the door flung open. What a surprise I had!

There stood a regal lady dog. She was white and fluffy, but not like Mom, more like a bear. She stood in the entryway like a guard, her sky blue eyes watching the area around her master, making sure he was safe from harm. She eyed me, up and

CousCous Mackey

down, and side to side. Her nose was twitching all the time, taking in my scent. She narrowed her eyes and lowered her head, quietly circling, viewing me from every angle. She never made a sound, but just breathed in and out, deeply and evenly. She reminded me of my Dad, the way he watched over my Mom and me as he sat outside our laundry room window.

There was no mistaking that this beautiful lady was in charge of the house, and if I wanted to belong, I would have to live by her laws.

She looked up at her master, as if to say, "Not so fast. I need a few minutes to make sure this little pup understands the rules."

They must have been together for a long time because he understood her body language perfectly. He closed the door and walked ahead, leaving the two of us behind.

I stood very still, trying to show my respect for her territory. After she made another circle, she slightly lifted her head and relaxed her shoulders. I took this signal to mean that, so far, I was okay. In response to her sign of welcome, I laid on my back, lifting my four short paws and showing her my tummy, meaning that I understood that this was her home and that I was here as her guest. She came over to me and gently licked my tummy and chest. Her touch was almost as soft and gentle as my Mom's. I sighed very deeply and small tears filled my eyes and began to run down the sides of my face.

In a calming voice, much too subtle for human ears to hear, she said, "Welcome to my home. My name is Sasha. You'll be safe here. And, there'll be plenty of time to let those tears out. But first, let me show you the rest of the house."

I stood up and shook myself off, and for the first time in

hours felt safe. And so, we went on our tour.

The inside of the house was much like the outside. All sorts of things were lying around here and there. My new friend, Sasha, explained to me that they had just moved to this house and that her master, Mr. Bill, was a bachelor. That meant a person who was not too neat and didn't have anyone to clean up after him.

Sasha said that she loved Mr. Bill very much, and that even though her meals weren't always on time, he was a very good and caring man who provided for lots of animals, but of course, loved her best. After being abandoned and homeless as a pup, Sasha was rescued by Mr. Bill and had been with him now for many years. They moved around to many houses, but Sasha said she never once worried about being put out by Mr. Bill. "After all," she said. "Who would take care of him?"

Travelling in Mr. Bill's small, blue car, was one of the best things, because the trip always ended up at a "food stop," and she got to eat things that most dogs didn't get, like donuts, hot dogs, chips, cookies, bacon, steaks, and Cokes. Boy, those sure kept her up at night! It wasn't easy to keep trim, at her age, but it was hard to say no to such tasty treats.

We walked around and I could pick up the scent of other animals, but I didn't know where or what they were. We went from room to room. The kitchen had half-empty boxes of pots and pans stacked around ready to be put away. Sasha said Mr. Bill would probably never put all the things away because it would be easier to pack for the next move. Used and clean dishes were piled in the sink next to a bowl of cereal. Large bottles of spring water were laid on their sides, propping up an old ironing board currently serving as the breakfast table.

There was a small room off the kitchen that had space for a washer and dryer, and for a box full of sand. Sasha said it was a litter box. I would later learn what that was for! There were several green garbage bags full of laundry. A large door, that had a little door in it, led to the backyard. Sasha said that the smaller door was for us to go in and out of. She wasn't too sure I was big enough to get through it, but she said not to worry because she would help me use it.

There were five more rooms. A small dining room housed a bicycle, sleeping bags, and two tires. There were two bedrooms, one with a computer and lots of sound equipment. The other had a big bed that jiggled when you jumped on it. Sasha said it was a waterbed and that we got to sleep on it whenever we wanted to. The living room had a sofa and two chairs that we were also allowed on, and a very large television. There were lots of other things, but it was hard to tell exactly what they were because shirts and jeans covered them. The last room was the bathroom. This room was very important because sometimes Sasha had to drink out of the large white standing-bowl that looked like a chair if Mr. Bill forgot to leave water for her.

We walked back into the kitchen to find Mr. Bill sitting on the end of the kitchen counter next to the side of the sink. He was holding something very fuzzy and round in his lap. It looked like a snow-white hairy ball. He had an opened Coke next to him. While he was rubbing the fuzzy ball, it made a strange, high-pitched, humming sound. Every so often the fuzzy white ball seemed to move and quiver, and get out of shape, but then it always went back into the shape of a ball.

Mr. Bill looked up at Sasha and me and with a very happy smile on his face said, "Well, Sash, have you taken care of our little girl here? I don't know what her name is, so I guess we're just gonna have to call her 'Little Girl,' that is, until we figure out something else."

In response to Mr. Bill's query, Sasha turned and picked me up by the scruff of my neck with her large mouth. She took me over to a large community water bowl and food plate, and placed me down. Then she laid down at the foot of the counter Mr. Bill was sitting on and continued to watch all the action. Mr. Bill went on rubbing the noisy, fuzzy white ball. At his feet, Sasha looked up at his fluffy companion, and said, "Snowflake, I want to introduce you to our newest roommate, Little Girl."

What a surprise I had when the furry white ball produced two small, folded over ears, sticking out of an oval face on one end, and a long, raccoon-like tail on the other. There were also four delicate legs, short like mine, but not curved like a Pekinese. What a change my life had taken. I now had a name, and had officially met my first cat.

"Hello, Snowflake," I said.

Snowflake jumped from Mr. Bill's lap with the grace and ease of an early fall leaf. She floated to the kitchen floor as though she were riding a breeze. When she reached the tiles she stretched out and, for a moment, it appeared as though she was twice her size. Then all of a sudden she returned to her original shape. Slowly, she

CousCous Mackey

placed her legs under her body and curled up next to me on the floor. Her tail was hidden somewhere beneath her. Only her small plump head and folded ears could be seen protruding from her white fluffy body. She stared directly into my eyes, never blinking, all the time wheezing a gentle steady hum. She remained as still as a statue.

Mr. Bill slid off the counter, taking his Coke with him. Sasha immediately went to his side. He knelt down and rubbed my head and scratched my ears. He transferred his attention to a sculpture-still Snowflake and gently stroked her to the rhythm of her wheeze. Snowflake blinked once and closed her eyes for good.

"You take a nap too, Little Girl. You've had a rough day."

I settled down next to a humming Snowflake, and she slowly slid her elasticized paw out from under her frame and placed it just under my nose. I closed my eyes and listened to her soft purring and, feeling her warm breath, imagined I was in my Mom's arms nestled next to her tummy and heart.

As Sasha and Mr. Bill walked away, I could hear him say, "She sure is a cute one, isn't she, Sash?"

And then he laughed and laughed and laughed. Mr. Bill had the happiest laugh I ever heard.

I hoped it was a sign of things to come.

CHAPTER 27

A Little Girl's Story

I hadn't slept for very long when I was aware of some newcomers in the kitchen. I opened my eyes to see four cats perched in various places throughout the room. Sasha was there, too, making sure that only Mr. Bill's cats wandered in and out of the doggie door.

One of the newcomers was mostly gray and had stripes all over—even over the spot covering his missing eye. Sasha said his name was One Eye. One Eye had been with them for about a year, now. It seems that a nasty neighbor of One Eye's was dead set against cats. No real reason, just didn't like them.

One Eye still tells the story. "Imagine my surprise. There I am, minding my own business, watching a plump little mouse, just ripe for the pickin's when the old neighbor calls me over. 'Meow, meow, little kitty. Here's a little treat.' So, am I stupid. You know

memory of the howls of my Dad, watching Mr. Granite's car as I was being driven away from my family.

With Sasha and all the cats gathered around me in the kitchen, I blurted out my story, or as much as I could remember. I was out of control. My tear soaked face was streaked with dust and gasoline. I told them about my Mom and Dad, Needles and his friends, and *The Humans.* I hung my head in despair, and yet felt a certain relief. All the time I talked, Sasha and the cats tried to console me, except the fourth cat, Oldtimer. He sat like a lamppost, listening intently to every detail of my adventure.

After I was through, everyone, well, almost everyone was just as exhausted from listening, as I was from talking. Sasha suggested that we all go to the waterbed for a good night's sleep. The only one not to join us was Oldtimer. He just quietly got up and left the house for the night. We heard Mr. Bill's car pull into the driveway as we jumped onto the waterbed, so even Sasha was able to relax for the few remaining hours before dawn.

When I woke up the next morning, it was not at all like when I lived with the Granites. I didn't have to hide or be real quiet and no one seemed to be the least bit worried about Mr. Bill hurting anyone in the house. The more I learned about Mr. Bill, the more I loved him. He shared his food and home with us, and most importantly, he shared his love.

The next few days I just rested and got used to the new routine. Mr. Bill was pretty busy because he was a schoolteacher. Sasha said he read a lot of books and did a lot of work on a computer. But even while he read and studied and worked on his computer, Mr. Bill always had time for us. Every day he would come home and hug and kiss us, especially Sasha, whom he loved in a very special way. He prepared our food, gave us water, and he made sure the doggie door did not get blocked by leaves and branches. The best thing though, was when Mr. Bill would give us one of the happiest laughs in the whole world. It would make the whole house shake.

🐾

CHAPTER 28

Friends in Deed

Learning about the other animals and the way they lived was so very interesting, and fun, too. Learning about new people was a different story. Except for Mr. Bill, my exposure to humans was not off to a very good start. I was beginning to wonder if maybe all humans were bad. But, Sasha assured me that there are good humans and bad humans, just like there are good animals and bad animals. Just like Mom, Sasha taught me many things.

It didn't take long for me to notice that Sasha did the same things every day, at just about the same time. I learned that this was called a routine, and that all good watchdogs needed to have one. "Everyone needs to have a routine to be successful," Sasha would say. "You need to be on time and be reliable. No lying in the sun until your job is done!" I replied, "Yes, M'am."

November came and went and I learned to do my chores first, very early in the day. Only then would I visit with yard friends and neighbors and nap in and out of the house. When Mr. Bill came home from school, it was time to start all over, and do our night patrol.

Each morning, we'd wake Mr. Bill by jumping up and down on the waterbed. We shook it until he rolled over and finally put his feet on the floor and headed for the bathroom. After he was *really* out of the bed we would each take a corner of his quilt in our mouths and shake our heads until the cover fell nice and smoothly over the bumpy mattress. Once the bed was made Sasha would go out the doggie door and then through the broken fence gate to get Mr. Bill's morning paper. (This she did alone, because, after all, she was the alpha dog.) Then, after Mr. Bill read through his newspaper and gulped down his coffee, he left for the day and we continued with our routine.

Sasha taught me how to push and nuzzle all of the doors and windows to keep them closed tight so that Mr. Bill's home was safe and sound. We did a kitchen check next. One of the cats (in this case, Snowflake) jumped to the shelf above the stove and sniffed for open gas jets. Oldtimer was usually responsible for making sure that the broken refrigerator door was closed shut. Finally, Sasha pushed her nose on the button sticking out of the small television Mr. Bill watched in the morning, making the picture go blank and the words stop coming out. Only when all of our work was done would we eat the leftovers Mr. Bill left for us on his plate and began our daily talks.

The cats, though, would go away from the house for hours at a time. They would always come home to eat their dinner, but during the day, Sasha said they went "catting" around. At night, when they returned from their social calls, they would tell Sasha and me about all the places they had been, and all the friends, old and new, they had met.

My friends asked me lots of questions about where I lived and how I happened to come to their home, too. It was hard to talk about at first, but in time, it became easier. Everyone was so kind that it made me feel good to share my stories with them. Little by little, when I was not so scared, I began to remember more things that I forgot to tell when I first arrived at the house.

One thing I could not tell my new friends, of course, was whether or not my Mom was still alive. It was something I dared not think of.

Then, in early December, after the cats had come home for the evening, Oldtimer came up to me and put his nose very close to mine. It was cold and damp and quivered just ever so slightly. His eyes seemed as large as saucers and the little diamond shaped slits in the middle slowly grew until they looked like large pools of dark water. He never blinked. He was breathing very softly, and with a humming wheeze, he said, "Little Girl, I have some news for you."

"For me, Mr. Oldtimer, news for me?"

I didn't know what to think.

"What is it, Mr. Oldtimer?" I asked.

Looking like the very wise old cat that he was, Oldtimer slowly began to speak.

"You know, Little Girl, I've lived in this neighborhood for many years now, and I have many, many friends. I have done many good deeds for these friends, and they have done many good deeds for me. Good deeds for each other, you know is what makes good friends. Several weeks ago, when you first came to be, I started to ask these many friends if anybody knew your Mom and Dad, this Feathers and Mr. Beaux. It took a while, but an old friend was brought to me who knows of your parents. Now, a lot of people think that cats and mice don't get along, but that's just a myth. All animals get along if people just leave them alone. Anyway, this friend of mine happens to be a mouse that lives near the Granite home. His name is Needles."

My heart was beating so fast and my tail wagging so quickly I could not stand still. Although I would never forget Uncle Needles, Aunt Bean and Uncle Willie, it was as though they were in another world, a world that I had been ripped away from. The pain of thinking about them was so great, I had all but obliterated them from my memory. But now, hearing Uncle Needles' name was like hearing my Mother's heartbeat for the first time. It filled me with life and hope.

"Please, oh please Mr. Oldtimer, please tell me about my Mom. Is she alive? I must know." I could not contain myself. "And my Dad, Mr. Beaux, is he still the most handsome dog in the world? Oh please, tell me."

"Let's see now," Oldtimer said, as he arched his body starting at the back of his neck and rolling to the tip of his tail. "Settle down there, Little Girl, and I'll tell you everything I can. Ah, yes, the most important news is that your Mother, Feathers, is alive. She's had a very hard time since you were taken away, and she's a very sick dog. But, the signs are good.

"*The Woman Human* threw Feathers into a dilapidated storage box, leaving her for dead, but thanks to one of Needles' cohorts, a Willie mouse, she was found and saved by this Beaux's human, BJ. Feathers lives with your Dad now. Her wounds from the Granites are improving nicely, but some say it is a broken heart that will not seem to heal. (You know, Little Girl, a broken heart is the hardest thing to mend.) She can't eat very much, and she stopped drinking water. Your Dad puts small drops of liquid on her tongue throughout the day, but some of her fluffy hair has fallen out and her once-sparkling eyes are very dull and cloudy. Needles said your Mom is slightly improved, but not knowing what happened to you occupies her mind all the time and she just can't seem to snap out of it. Your Dad, Beaux, is holding on just to take care of her. But he, too, has a heavy heart."

Just hearing that Mom was alive made my head swim. For weeks I dared not think about her or Dad, or our brief life together. All my images of my Mom took me to that terrible moment in the laundry room. And thinking of my Dad and his plaintive howls, as I vainly peered from the passenger seat of Mr. Granite's car—these images were too cruel. I had to shut them out.

Knowing that Mom was alive, and living with Dad, was more than I had ever prayed for. My legs began to hop up and down as if on their own. I twirled and turned, finally dizzily falling on the floor in the middle of the kitchen floor.

"Mr. Oldtimer, Mr. Oldtimer," I stammered. "How can I ever thank you for such wonderful news? How can you ever know what it means to me?" As I went on with my thanks and more questions, Mr. Oldtimer's eyes blinked once and as though a magical trance had ended, his pupils quickly became thin slits, and he turned and jumped to his refrigerator perch. "There's no more to tell, Little Girl. There's no more to tell."

In some ways, my life was now much easier. In other ways it was much worse. Knowing my Mom was alive, and with my Dad, brought me tremendous joy. But knowing that my parents were together, without me, also brought me tremendous pain.

Before Mr. Oldtimer's message, I would allow myself to imagine (just a little bit at a time), Mom and Dad being gone from me forever. It was very hard, but it was final. Now, I could not rest just imagining that there was even the slightest possibility of us being reunited. All my waking hours were consumed with only one thought. *How could we be a family again?*

I ached for my Mom's touch and scent.

Sometimes, at night, when it was clear and crisp and the moon was like a big ball in the sky, I would go to the farthest corner of the yard, in the direction Mr. Oldtimer said my parents lived, and together with Sasha, we would howl and bark messages that I prayed my Mom and Dad would receive.

Mr. Oldtimer said that he had sent word back through Uncle Needles that I was alive and living in a safe home. Still, I longed to hear my Mom's and Dad's barks and howls for myself.

CHAPTER 29

For Once Good News Travels Fast!

When Uncle Needles returned home to tell of his meeting with Mr. Oldtimer, Dad could not believe his ears.

"It's your typical good news, bad news story, Beaux. Your pup is alive, and presumably well. Livin' with a dude named Bill. A good guy, as humans go. That's the good news."

"Now, now, Needles," Dad said. "You know, we've been getting false sightings for weeks now. You know how hard that is on Feathers and me. Is this a reliable cat? Do you think our baby *IS* truly alive? And if she is, what could possibly be *the bad news?*"

"Well, let me tell you, pal. Reliable cat? (Some would say that's a contradiction in terms.) But yeah, this guy's the real McCoy. Top choice. He ain't been ruined by them humans who makes cats and dogs and mice and stuff chase each other around and all that rough stuff. He's legit. If he says your gal is okay, she's okay. The bad news is, she's across the freeway! That's why we lost her scent the way we did. Once she got into them car fumes and truck wind, all that fast traffic and such, her scent was gone. We know where she is, but gettin' her ain't gonna be that easy."

"Across the freeway! Well, it all makes sense now. All the neighborhood patrols. Even the flyers can't cross that wind tunnel. All that smoke going up, clogging the air? Across the freeway! Well, we'll have to come up with something. Feathers and I will just have to figure something out."

"I don't know, pal. Think Feathers is ready to hear this? Maybe we should just wait it out a bit, check this a little longer?"

"No, Needles. It's tempting, but no. Feathers has a right to every bit of information, even the hurtful kind. I just pray this time it is not a false rumor, and that we can come up with a plan to get our little girl back."

"Yeah, well, me too, big guy!"

In telling me his version of the story, Dad said that as usual, you can never be prepared for a female's reaction to anything. He said this is true no matter what the species. When he told Mom of Uncle Needles' meeting with Mr. Oldtimer, Mom's reaction was not at all what he had expected.

As coolly and calmly as can be, Mom said, "Well then, I suppose we'd better get ready for our baby's return. It is time I started to pull myself together so that I can manage a growing pup." Dad did not know what to make of Mom's complete confidence in my ultimate return.

"Feathers, did you understand the part about the freeway?

You haven't had that much experience with it," Dad said. "You know I'm not afraid of very much and that I'd give my life to bring our girl home. I think I could probably come up with a pretty good plan to get me across but—it's the coming back. I would rather know our baby was healthy and happy without us, then risk her life crossing that treacherous road!"

"Beaux," Mom said, firmly. "We will get our little girl back. I don't know how, not yet, but I beg you to trust in my faith. Our little girl will come home."

The change in their spirits, and so of course, their health, was so abrupt that BJ did not know what to make of it. Mom's appetite, all but a memory, returned overnight. Dad's patrols, infrequent at best, started up as though he had never missed a beat.

When BJ discovered Mom and Dad eagerly standing at the back gate with their leashes in their mouths, indicating that a walk was being requested, she could not have been happier, if somewhat confused.

What a pleasure and relief she felt to see Mom and Dad sitting in the backyard, warming themselves in the early winter sun, vigorously howling into the oncoming breeze.

Even though BJ is as astute a human as possible, she was unaware of the communications that were going on between Mom and Dad and their neighborhood animal-internet. Word of my survival spread through the pet vine, fueling Mom's confidence in someday getting me back. She did not know how it would happen, but she would spend the rest of her life trying. Like any Mom, she had to.

Dad's response to the news granted him a new life, too. He was still skeptical about how the miracle might happen, but seeing Mom back on her feet and learning that I had made it safely out of Mr.

Granite's grip, gave him the will to hold on—at least a little longer.

He was determined to pull out all the stops to get me back. Considering all that he and Mom had overcome, he began to believe they could accomplish this, too!

Humans have their own communication tools, and BJ and Mr. Bill had not been sitting idle. Although their lifestyles were quite different and they lived on opposite sides of town, each was busy posting notices about a lost and found puppy.

Almost from the time I came to live with him and Sasha, Mr. Bill began putting up signs around the nearby convenience stores, the neighborhood bars and local Mexican restaurants. His notice read:

> *FOUND: The most beautiful puppy in the world. Soft fluffy hair, great disposition. A real gem. Caller must prove ownership. Will not give up without PROOF OF OWNERSHIP!!!*

Then he listed his name and telephone number.

BJ, too, was busy posting bulletins throughout her neighborhood, and at local stores and gas stations that she frequented. Friends and workers at the Whole Foods Market put flyers into grocery bags. She called all the local veterinary clinics on her side of town, and her neighborhood police station was supplied with handouts saying:

> *LOST: Precious little puppy. Peach colored. Cute as a button. Please call BJ with information. LARGE REWARD. VERY LARGE REWARD!*

Then she listed her telephone number. But, living across the freeway, in such different worlds, their handbills never crossed. Although Mr. Bill and BJ were diligent about replacing torn-up notices, even they began to think that I would never be reunited with my family. As time went on my fondness for Mr. Bill and Sasha and all the cats and other new friends I had made grew, and while my heart was still aching, the pain began to dull.

Christmas was right around the corner, and other responsibilities began to take over.

Mom and Dad, however, had no other agenda, so unbeknownst to me, things were not really dying down. Taking first things first, Mom continued to build up her strength. She knew she'd have to be fit to raise a growing puppy, once she got me home.

Dad did what Dads do best. He took charge. He immediately dispatched Uncle Needles to track down Mr. Oldtimer. He wanted to send his gratitude and his respect. He knew he'd be indebted to Mr. Oldtimer for life and he needed to acknowledge the debt. It was the right thing to do, even in the animal world.

Uncle Needles was eager to deliver the message to his old friend and he even toyed with the idea of visiting Mr. Bill's place himself, but Mr. Oldtimer gave warnings dissuading him of such thoughts.

"Needles, it's a New World out there," he said. "I have pretty good control over the brood at Mr. Bill's, but there's a whole neighborhood of young Turks still needing to earn their whiskers. I don't doubt for one minute they'd like to notch their tails with a catch like you. They're freeway savvy and you're not. It's not that far, as the crow flies, but I grab a lift from one of the delivery trucks that crosses that sea of traffic everyday. They're a lot more accommodating to an old graying cat than they would be to a shaggy old mouse—no offense meant!"

That was all Uncle Needles needed to hear.

"No offense taken, pal. I got the picture. None of us is as young as we used to be, eh. Just tell that little gal that ol' Uncle Needles is looking forward to the day she comes home. And ask her to tell you about them first steps I helped her take. And Oldtimer, Mr. Beaux's word is his bond. You made a good friend, for life. You can bank on it."

CHAPTER 30

No Food's Like Whole Foods

Christmas break came and Mr. Bill was able to spend more time at home. He loved putting up the big old-fashioned lights inside and out, making the house glow. He played and sang along to Christmas music, and then he'd take a break and venture all over the city to do his holiday shopping.

He explored new shops and restaurants that he had learned of from fellow teachers and even his students, always bringing home exotic new treats that we would taste-test. Some of them, of course, would surely give Sasha and me an upset stomach, but still we were never able to refuse. Today it was fruitcake and eggnog. What a delicious combination.

It was Snowflake who spied them first. She was wrestling with three of the visiting cats to get into the grocery bag that some of the eggnog had dripped into. The bag, lying on the floor, was begging for their exploration.

Mr. Bill didn't often shop at fancy specialty stores, but for Christmas he indulged the entire household. Everyone got a treat. For himself he bought a huge steak, a big potato just aching to be baked, and lots of fresh salad. "All organic," he kept saying. "No matter how much we eat, we can't get sick!" The fruitcake and eggnog were for Sasha and me, after we finished with Mr. Bill's dinner leftovers. (Although in truth there wasn't too much of Mr. Bill's dinner left.) There were several pounds of fresh shrimp for all the cats. Plus, of course, the bag to play in.

Sasha and I had just finished a slice of moist fruitcake and were about to get into licking a plastic container with just the smallest remnants of peanut butter. (We decided to save the eggnog for our midnight treat.)

"Hey, Sasha, Little Girl, come over here," Snowflake said. "Look here, there are some papers stuffed at the bottom of this bag and I think they're talking about you, Little Girl. It must be you, you're the only dog I know of that looks like a peach. I mean, a good peach, of course," Snowflake added.

Sasha snatched one of the papers from Snowflake's paws.

"Let's see that. What have you got there?" Looking at the notice Sasha exclaimed, "Oh my, Little Girl, I *do* think this is you. It's a notice about a missing puppy. A puppy that looks like a peach."

Almost at once, everyone took in a deep breath, and for just a second, a hush fell over the room.

This was not the first notice BJ had sent out, but having received no response to her earlier queries, she had decided it would be the last. Sasha somberly read it:

> *TO WHOM IT MAY CONCERN:*
>
> *LAST HALLOWEEN OUR PRECIOUS LITTLE PUPPY WAS TAKEN AWAY FROM US. SHE WAS ONLY FOUR WEEKS OLD, AND LOOKED VERY MUCH LIKE A SOFT PEACH. IF YOU HAVE SEEN HER, OR KNOW OF HER WHEREABOUTS, PLEASE HELP HER COME BACK TO HER FAMILY. WE MISS HER VERY MUCH. PLEASE MAKE OUR CHRISTMAS COMPLETE AND RETURN OUR LITTLE GIRL TO HER HOME. A LARGE REWARD, PLUS OUR DEEPEST GRATITUDE, IS OFFERED FOR HER SAFE RETURN. THIS WILL BE OUR LAST NOTICE!*

It was signed—*From the Family of BJ, Mr. Beaux and Feathers.* An address and telephone number followed. The crowd became as quiet as only Uncle Needles, Aunt Bean, and Uncle Willie can be. The silence drummed in my ears. The playful cats left the Whole Foods bag in the center of the floor and quietly climbed to their nests.

I was still not a very experienced reader, so I asked Sasha to go over the notice again. When she was done, she quietly said, "Snowflake is right, Little Girl. This is definitely a plea from your family. I guess we'd better make sure Mr. Bill sees it."

Sasha took the notice and, walking very slowly, placed it near one of her old, worn-out blankets. Then, we laid down and snuggled closely for the night.

The next morning, December 23, was cold and crisp. No matter what, we still had jobs to do. We got up very early, almost before the light, and, without waking the cats, softly climbed through the doggie door to see the sun rise.

Like my Mom, I have always loved the mornings best. They are full of hope. But this December morning I was very confused. Seeing the notice sent out by BJ filled my heart with joy, but seeing Sasha's face and the expression of the household cats when they read the notice made me very sad.

All night long I dreamed of finally getting to see my Mom and Dad. But then, thoughts of saying goodbye to Mr. Bill and all my new friends, especially Sasha and Mr. Oldtimer, confused me. Thanks to Mr. Oldtimer and Uncle Needles, I knew that Mom and Dad were safe, and happy. Also because of them, Mom and Dad knew that I was safe.

I had grown to love my new family. I couldn't imagine knowingly hurting any one of them. I could only think that my heart must have grown very large in the last few hours, because it was so heavy in my chest I could hardly breathe.

Mr. Bill got home late the night before and would be sleeping for some time to come. Sasha and I used this time to talk and visit, and plan our day. With the sun just coming up over the far-off trees, Sasha said, "Well, Little Girl, I guess we'd better get that notice and take it into Mr. Bill's bedroom. If we don't hit him over

CousCous Mackey

the head with it, he'll likely not see it. I figure that if you jump up on the waterbed closest to his head, and I jump on his stomach, he'll leap up at us, like he always does when we wake him, and I can make sure I have the notice in my mouth. That way, when he tries to grab us for our morning tickle, he'll be sure to see it."

I couldn't help but hear the sad tone in Sasha's voice and see the long creases and the puffiness in her eyes. I replied, "You know, Sasha, I was thinking. Mr. Bill really has been working hard lately, and maybe we shouldn't bother him very early today. I think he needs to be able to sleep in for once. We can show him the notice a little later in the day, or maybe even tomorrow morning. We've got lots of time. What'd ya think?"

A huge smile broke out on Sasha's face, and she looked straight into my eyes. "Now, you think hard about this, Little Girl. We can wake him right now if you like."

Her spirits had risen so much, I knew I was right when I said, "No, no. Let's just wait a bit. We've got lots of time."

By now the sun had risen. Looking into the clear sky, Sasha said, "My goodness. It seemed so gloomy this morning, but what a wonderful day it is turning out to be."

CHAPTER 31

Fond Memories of Christmas Past

Things were not quite as calm and quiet at Mom and Dad's home. Christmas was a favorite time for BJ and her family, too. This morning she was busy making preparations for tomorrow's Christmas Eve dinner. She had lots of last-minute shopping before she could begin to prepare for the family feast.

Although a time of exchanging gifts and attending parties, for BJ's family it was mostly a time of thanks and sharing long-standing traditions. Her favorite was the "food exchange."

Many years ago a family friend invited for Christmas Eve dinner brought with him a dish from his native country very far away in Eastern Europe. He presented his dish to the family, and then shared his vivid memories of his family's Christmas rituals back in Warsaw many years ago. He told stories of handmade toy soldiers carved by his grandfather, and homemade pastries lovingly prepared by his grandmother. He also told of the hardships in celebrating the holiday because his family was very poor. BJ was just a young girl when this happened, but her memories of the strange food, and the stories by the mysterious guest, stuck with her throughout the years. When she was old enough to start her own holiday customs, each year she asked one guest to bring a food from a foreign land, along with stories of that country's holiday traditions. This year John and Deborah were elected to bring a "foreign dish," and BJ was just as excited to learn what it was, as when she was a child. The dish was always a surprise, and the stories always a delight.

As she sorted through all her Christmas shopping lists, BJ came upon her last notice seeking information about my whereabouts and felt a deep sense of regret. She had so hoped her efforts would have proved fruitful, and that she could have reunited Mom and Dad with their puppy. But over the last several weeks, with the urgency the holidays create, the calls of false sightings and sincere animal helpers had all but stopped. This notice, distributed a few days before, was going to have to be the last effort.

The recent change she sensed in Mom and Dad had convinced her that they were getting over their loss and she hoped marked a turning point in their recoveries. Mom and Dad certainly acted like they felt better, and seemed almost 100%.

Even for an avid animal lover like BJ, her inherent humanness would never allow her to fully understand the change in Mom and Dad. I guess we can never really understand someone else's suffering.

BJ had no way of knowing that the return of Mom's grooming regimen was not being done so she could enjoy her warm, soft coat. She had no way of knowing that Mom thought only of wrapping me in her arms and letting me rest my head near her tummy and heart, like we did so long ago. Mom and Dad were not thriving because they were getting over me; they were thriving in preparation for my return.

It was true that time was running out, and all the holiday traffic made it more difficult for the neighborhood animals to safely roam the alleys and parking lots, so there was no recent word from Oldtimer. But, it was Christmas for Mom and Dad, too, and they refused to give up their hope for a miracle.

While both BJ and Mr. Bill prepared themselves for the next day's Christmas Eve events, Mr. Oldtimer returned home, frustrated that he was not able to connect again with Uncle Needles.

"Where do all these humans come from? They're like roaches crawling out of the woodwork. They interfere with all the parking and deliveries. I couldn't get to my truck today because a car full of shoppers insisted on stopping right in the spot with all the yellow lines. It's the only place an old cat like me can easily get onto the truck bumper. I'll be glad when these holidays are over." And then, quite facetiously, "Hum-bug!"

Getting no reaction from Snowflake and the other visiting cats, Mr. Oldtimer inquired as to the blue mood in the kitchen. Snowflake gingerly passed Mr. Oldtimer the worn notice. After he read the crumbled paper found in the shopping bag, he, too, could feel the weight of a goodbye in his heart.

December twenty-third was one of the longest days of my life. Most of us had finally gone to bed when Mr. Oldtimer found

Sasha quietly sitting at the front entry hall, watching for Mr. Bill. He was more than shocked to hear Sasha tell him of my decision *not* to give the circular to Mr. Bill.

Suddenly, Mr. Oldtimer noticed that Sasha looked quite old and fragile. Although she outweighed Mr. Oldtimer by at least fifty pounds, he sensed her vulnerability and loneliness. He gently glided up to her and placed his hefty paws on Sasha's head and said, "Sasha, surely you must know that we have got to help Little Girl get home. She is only trying to avoid more pain in her young life by not having to say another goodbye. You can see, I'm sure, that she loves us very dearly, almost as much as we love her." Then, his voice breaking, and his whiskers drooping low to the ground, he continued, "Love, Sasha, true love, is letting go. We must get Little Girl home."

Without another word, Oldtimer returned to his kitchen perch. When he nestled his worn face deep into his belly we could not tell if the muffled sounds coming from his body were purrs or sobs. No one wanted to ask.

After Mr. Bill arrived home, Sasha returned to the kitchen and looked at the other cats, the youngsters, knowing most of them had been discarded like so much excess garbage. She remembered her own abandonment, and the deep pain she carried. Even her years with Mr. Bill could not make her forget all the hurt. She walked through the house, making her last patrol for the night, when she happened upon me, silently snuggled up to my favorite toy: a shaggy, moth eaten, partially disintegrated feather duster. Sasha knew then what she had to do.

🐾

CHAPTER 32

'Twas the Night Before Christmas

On December twenty-fourth, Christmas Eve morning, Sasha and I got up as usual. But, after just a few moments in the cold morning mist, Sasha said, "Little Girl, how about if I go into the house to get an old bone to chew on while the sun comes up over the trees?" Agreeing to keep an eye on the yard (knowing full well she never failed to bring me a treat, too), Sasha went back into the house.

My memory of that morning, sitting alone in the chilly dew, has never faded. I knew that my Mom was as close to me as she had ever been—I was certain of it. I whispered an almost silent goodbye to her, and Dad, hoping that they would approve of my decision to show my gratitude to Sasha and Mr. Bill by staying with them for-ever. My howls were weak, but the love in them so strong that, several miles away, also sitting in the rays of the rising sun, my Mom jumped to her feet and ran in agitated circles around her yard. Of course, she could not tell anyone of the dark premonition she had just had. "No, no," she thought. "This cannot be! Not on Christmas Eve."

Meanwhile, Sasha was trying the impossible.

Mr. Bill, being out late the night before, was not easily awakened. With the soggy, tattered notice in her mouth, Sasha jumped on the waterbed and began to cause a small tidal wave. Mr. Bill reached out and attempted to rub her tummy, a sure way to calm her. She continued to pounce, whining and snorting at the same time. He put a large pillow over his head and turned over in the warm bed. Sasha would have to try later. She carefully took the notice and, trying to straighten it out with her paws, slid it under the quilt. Returning to the yard, she offered me an old soup bone that she had retrieved from last night's dinner. Lying down on the soft grass, she said, "Merry Christmas, Little Girl."

CousCous Mackey

CHAPTER 33

How Quickly Time Flies...

Sasha went to check on Mr. Bill several times during the early morning, but try as she might, he would not budge. "Sash, it's the principle of the thing. It is my Christmas break, and Christmas Eve to boot. I'm sleeping in!"

By mid-afternoon, Sasha was concerned that she might back out of her commitment to help me get back to my family. If she were going to go through with her plan she would have to take drastic measures. Marching into Mr. Bill's bedroom, she jumped up on the bed and, baring her teeth, took a large bite out of the middle of the mattress. Within seconds a veritable geyser was gushing from Mr. Bill's bed. The water hit him in the face, and then continued to run down the length of his body, surrounding him in a pool of warm liquid.

Sasha, having retrieved the notice from under the quilt, stood over Mr. Bill until he finally awoke from his stupor. Feeling the water covering his body, he jumped out of bed in a disoriented hysteria and shouted out to Sasha.

"Hurry girl, I'll save you! It's flooding all around us. Quick, get Little Girl and the cats. We'll have to find a boat."

Sasha just shrugged her shoulders in frustration and stood her ground. Coming to, Mr. Bill realized that the rising water was confined to his bed, and blurted out a list of questions. "Sasha, what's going on, what have you done, you could have just called me, you didn't have to try and drown me, what could be so important?" Finally Mr. Bill noticed the shredded paper hanging from the corner of Sasha's mouth. He took it from her jaw, salvaging the moist pieces.

"Oh my, Sasha, do you see what this says? It's about our Little Girl. Her family is trying to find her. Oh, Sasha, our Little Girl is going to have to go home."

Sasha turned from the room and walked to the kitchen. She lay down on the floor and closed her eyes, even though she was not the slightest bit sleepy.

Mr. Bill flew into the bathroom and decided that, since he was all wet anyway, he may as well take a shower. He quickly washed, talking to himself the whole time.

"Let's see, now. I'll have to call first to make sure that it is the right home. No, no, I don't want to call. I want to see the place for myself. I'm not just gonna turn our Little Girl over to someone without making sure their house is fit to raise such a good little puppy. I'll circle the block, making sure everything is okay...."

And on and on his thoughts went.

After the shower, he went to the kitchen and discretely spoke to Sasha. Of course, Oldtimer could hear every word.

"Sasha, now don't say anything to Little Girl. If this is a false alarm I don't want to upset her. I'll handle this. We'll all do a little ride-by. If it looks okay, then we'll see what happens. But, we're not giving up our baby to just anyone."

Mr. Bill left the room to continue dressing. Oldtimer arose from the refrigerator and jumped to the floor. He walked up to Sasha and said, "Merry Christmas, Sasha. Merry Christmas."

Without another sound, he walked out of the doggie door.

Part V

It's love, it's love that makes the world go round.

—Anon
(Used by W.S. Gilbert
in *Iolanthe*)

CHAPTER 34

The Final Preparations are Made

The day was passing quickly at Mom and Dad's, too. Family and guests were arriving and the house was decorated inside and out.

Dad had on his dark green leather collar with small silver bells imbedded in it. Mom had a beautiful red velvet bow loosely tied around her neck. Her sheen had returned to her coat and her eyes were clear and sparkling. She had managed to brush off her disturbing morning thoughts. Generous as always, she and Dad took several of their treats to share with Uncle Needles, Uncle Willie and Aunt Bean, who were comfortably settled under a pile of clean, sweet smelling Christmas boxes, originally bearing cookies and nuts. Several of the boxes had gotten a pretty rough ride over their delivery path, and some of the insides had broken apart, leaving wonderful bits and morsels for the mice. Oh, what a wonderful Christmas it was going to be.

No one mentioned me, and Dad was a little apprehensive about Mom's upbeat mood. With so much time having passed since I was taken away, and no recent word from Mr. Oldtimer, Dad was no longer as confident about my return. Bringing up the subject to Mom was out of the question. He thought for sure she would take a nosedive. He knew her only reason for continuing with such a full recovery was because of her belief that I would soon be returned to them. And, it was Christmas and he was not about to put a damper on anyone's spirits, so he just went along with the good mood and all the family fun.

He had always been included in the festivities, and having Mom with him this year was going to make it a wonderful holiday. Even though his hopes of being reunited were waning, he could not help but be thankful knowing of my safety.

He prepared to do his last rounds for the night, but before he went through the doggie door, he took another look at his beautiful home, and his beautiful Feathers.

The living room was a living garden. The Christmas tree stood at least eight feet tall and was covered with toys of all sizes, shapes, and shades. BJ had collected them throughout the years, and some had been given to her as gifts. Many were made with pictures of family members on them, enclosed in miniature gilded frames. There were several of Dad at different ages. And this year, for the first time, there was a picture of Mom framed in a small green shiny ornament. Of course, there was also one of Mom and Dad together, in a delicate crystal frame.

Looking at Mom, he thought, "Oh my, she is so beautiful."

His lovely Feathers. Topping off the tree was a white angel, puffy and soft. (Dad said it made him think of me.)

The tables and bookshelves were adorned with nativity scenes from around the world. Christmas books were being reminisced over, with a hum of holiday music in the background. Poinsettias of every color and every shape added to the mood as well as garland draped around the fireplace, with small blinking lights interwoven in its needles.

Presents overflowed in stockings, in boxes, and in decorated bags with matching tissue paper billowing out.

The kitchen was a sea of the most delectable blended aromas, and *even* Dad knew the menu. There was turkey and ham, mashed potatoes, gravy, rice, stuffing, green beans, and a host of salads. For dessert, a pumpkin pie sat on a red and gold paper doily, with snow-flake-like cutouts throughout its design. And there were candies, holiday cookies, tarts, and special handmade dog biscuits. They had everything.

Dad didn't know what this year's surprise dish was going to be, but he hoped it would be better than last year's. Everyone else seemed to like it, but he wasn't really partial to olives. The little black and green balls with the stones inside were not much to his liking.

He had to admit, they had looked beautiful, swimming in a crystal dish with little silver stars and gold flowers on the outside of it. And when they were served, Dr. Dorothy, the lady who brought them, told a story about a country called Israel with a city named Jerusalem, where Jesus was born. It was all very meaningful, he was sure, but not too tasty to suit Dad.

The year Jean-Claude was chosen to bring the "mystery food" he brought a whole bunch of wonderful cheeses from France, the country where he was born. Oh, there was a good story with that food, too. And the cheeses *were* very much to Dad's liking.

This year, Uncle John and Aunt Deborah had brought a big red dish filled with something fluffy and light that looked like bits of rice. Except this food wasn't only white, like rice. It was also a very light peach color, like flecks of a soft sunrise. Like fluffy sunshine. It was a beautiful food, and Dad was anxious to find out its name and have a taste of it. Aunt Deborah said it came from a country far away, and she was going to tell a story about Christmas in that part of the world. It was hard to contain the feelings of excitement in the house.

Dad explored the dining room. It was definitely the most beautiful room of all. It was shaped like a biscuit-box, with two long sides, and two shorter sides, and it had four doors leading to other places. One went to the kitchen where all the food was being prepared, and one went to living room where children shook boxes, poked at bags trying to guess what treasures they held, and petted Mom and scratched her ears. Two large glass doors led to the outside, and overlooked the big water oak tree that Dad, and now Mom, rested under during the daytime hours. Tonight the tree was glittering with miniature lights and dozens of large colorful balls. Dad always had to clear his throat and blink his eyes when the table was set like this and the candles were just ready to be lit. He imagined what it would be like to have everyone in their seats, passing the food and sharing their love. How wonderful it was to be part of this family. His heart ached for me.

At dinnertime, a most special time, Mom and Dad would be seated on their separate cushions, right in front of the two large glass doors. Dad, of course, would be watching for intruders, while Mom would enjoy a view of the outside lights.

Family and friends walked throughout the house, putting more gifts under the tree, setting more pretty dishes on the dining room table, and stirring steaming pots in the kitchen.

Dad stopped at the salmon-colored brocade love seat, and seeing Mom seated there, he walked over to rub her nose before going outside for his last patrol of the day.

She looked into his eyes and said, "It was only in my most secret dreams that I ever imagined a Christmas like this. Even when the Granites were at their very best, my holidays were spent waiting for cold and often spoiled leftovers. I can remember hearing all of the activity in other parts of the house and just aching to be a part of the festivities. But, Mrs. Granite never wanted dog hair on her red velvet dress!"

"Well, my dear Feathers," Dad merrily said. "Now you have your very own red velvet bow, and how beautiful it looks in your soft, yellow hair!"

And then, almost in unison they said, "Merry Christmas."

There was no hint of despair in Mom's voice. And, of course, Dad did want to mar her newfound peacefulness, so he just hid his apprehension and aching heart.

CHAPTER 35

🐾

Dashing Through the Snow

M r. Bill paced. Up and back. Back and up. He would stop mid-step and then start out again. He walked from room to room, in and out. He knew what needed to be done, but he couldn't seem to muster up the courage to do it.

The thought of losing Sasha—and then someone finding her and not returning her to him—made him shiver. On the other hand, he had to wonder what kind of people would let such a precious little puppy get lost in the first place. What was he to do?

This was going to be one of the hardest decisions of his life.

As he stalked through the house and gathered the Christmas gifts he needed to deliver that night, he happened to stop near an open door to one of the side rooms. There I was, inside, lying quietly on my feather duster and a crumbled piece of paper. As Mr. Bill

Memoirs of a Dog   187

got closer, he saw my small, dried teardrops all over BJ's last notice. Mr. Bill did not need to see anymore. Instead he flew into gear.

Just as Mom had predicted many weeks ago, it had turned out to be a hard winter. The days were sunny, clear and cold. But, by the time the evening came the temperature was only in the high thirties, and there were even rumors (and to some, hopes) of possible light snow flurries.

Mr. Bill was ready to go. He had packed the car, brushed Sasha and me, and placed special Christmas treats around the house for all the cats. Just like he did as a little boy, he also put out a plate of cookies and a large glass of milk. After all, why tempt fate! Letting out a huge roar, he said to Sasha and me, "Well old girls, there's no need to laugh. I know it's just a silly old tradition, but it *is* a tradition! Besides, by the time we get home it'll give us something to snack on, unless of course...." He cut off his thought with another huge laugh.

"Okay, ladies, after you." Sasha, as always, loved to take rides with Mr. Bill. She got to sit in the seat next to him, peering out of the fingerprinted window, looking at all the interesting sights. She especially liked driving around during the holidays. She loved to see the brightly decorated homes and all of the people bustling around. I was learning to love it, too, and it was a lot more fun knowing that I was not going to be thrown out in the middle of the road when the ride was over. I was so small, Sasha let me share the seat she was in, which made it just that much cozier. It was also easier for us to check out all the neighborhood pets, hailing as we drove along.

Mr. Bill opened the car door, and Sasha and I jumped in. I had to take a few extra steps as usual, but Mr. Bill's car was pretty close to the ground, so it was not too hard for me to get up into the seat. As I snuggled next to Sasha, my sadness began to go away.

Mr. Bill was looking at a large sheet of paper in a very intent way. It was crunched up and wrinkled and when he was done with it, try as he might, he could not seem to tell which side was up. He just laughed that wonderful hearty laugh, and balled the paper up and threw it in the back seat.

"Oh, what the heck, Sash, old gal. If we get lost, we'll just ask for directions. Who needs a silly map, anyway?" There it was again, that laugh.

Mr. Bill turned on the car radio. He adjusted it to a station playing Christmas music. As a soft mist began to settle on the windshield, he turned on the heater. The warm air stirred Sasha's and my coat. I couldn't quite understand, then, the intent way Sasha kept looking at me.

Although we had to go into some very busy traffic and cross some very busy streets, the ride did not take too much time. Mr. Bill sang all the way, ad-libbing with hums and bongs when he didn't know all the words. Sasha and I tried to help by bobbing our heads in time to the music.

When we came to an area that was very quiet and where the homes were much larger than Mr. Bill's, the car came to an abrupt stop. Mr. Bill and Sasha peered out of the window. We were in front of a very lovely home that looked somewhat familiar to me, but I really didn't know why. Lights covered the outside trees and wreaths were hung on several large windows. Glowing candles, placed inside green bags with cut-out stars, lined the walkway to the house. Mr. Bill bent over the car seat and gently took me in his arms. He reached to the back of the car and pulled out a large red bow, which he placed around my neck. Large drops of water were forming in his eyes as he opened the car door and the harsh wind hit his face. Looking at Sasha, he said, "It's just the wind, old girl, just the wind." For once, there was no laugh. Sasha, holding back *her* tears, knew better.

We all got out of the car and began to walk up the brick path—I, in Mr. Bill's arms, and Sasha at our side. Mr. Bill could hear the sounds of cheering and clapping coming from inside. He said to himself, "Maybe these people aren't so bad, after all."

He then lifted me to his face and looked close into my eyes. He touched his nose to mine and softly placed his lips on my forehead. I felt several moist droplets hit my head.

Next, I heard a loud chiming sound in the tune of "I'll Be Home for Christmas."

CHAPTER 36

It's CousCous for Christmas

Dad's rounds were over and dinner was just about ready to be served. All the family and friends began to gather in the dining room, looking for their names on the cards shaped like Santa Claus, which sat on each gold rimmed plate. There was so much to take in. Children were being urged to leave the wrapped boxes and billowy bags under the tree.

Gammy Lil shed her knitted sweater, which covered a pretty holiday blouse decorated with teddy bears and silver and gold appliques. Sybil adjusted her printed socks and short skirt. Will and Andy had to be pried from their computer game, and Uncle Tom removed his apron and brought in a large bowl of salad. Uncle Dave kept the attention of young Wilem by letting him press the middle of his holiday tie, which then played brief rendition of "Jingle Bells."

When everyone took their assigned seats, BJ took Uncle Frank's hand on one side, and Aunt Alice's on the other. After that, all the family and guests held hands, too.

"It's time, it's finally time," BJ said. Then, when they all bowed their heads, some closing their eyes as well, she said a thank you prayer for all the good health and blessings they had received that day, and throughout the year.

During the prayer, Mom and Dad rested their paws together, while BJ placed her fuzzy Christmas slippers on their blanket. Mom couldn't help notice how many pairs of new shiny shoes were gathered under the table. What a big family she now had.

When the prayer was over, BJ said, "Okay everyone, it's time for our traditional Christmas dish and holiday story. Come on, John and Deborah, don't let us down." Smiling brightly, Aunt Deborah quickly left the room with Uncle John close behind. Whispers could be heard from the kitchen. Then, Uncle John returned and further dimmed the crystal chandelier. Suddenly, the glow in the room came from the bevy of candles places among the holiday feast. Almost magically, Aunt Deborah reappeared, carrying the glistening red bowl centered on a round silver tray.

As the entire table let out a collective sigh, Mom scurried between the matching shoes beneath the table and placed herself halfway up the entry hall stairway, giving her, for once, a bird's eye view of the events. Dad, of course, could see perfectly well from where he was, but chose to escort Mom to her perch.

After the oouus and aahhs subsided, the bowl was placed in the middle of the table for all the guests to see.

"Oh look, it's pink rice," one of the children said.

"No, no," said another. "It's Christmas grits."

"Well, you're both wrong," said Aunt Deborah. "This is a dish Uncle John and I learned about this past summer when we traveled to the Middle East. Does anyone else have any guesses?"

After a few moments of silence, Uncle John piped in.

"This dish is called couscous, and it is from a country with holiday traditions very different from ours."

Immediately, Mom thought to herself, "What a beautiful name! It sounds like a song."

How light and fluffy it was, too. And when the candlelight hit it at an angle, it took on the hue of a pale peach.

And so, as the food was being passed and the Christmas Eve dinner enjoyed, Uncle John and Aunt Deborah began the Christmas tale about how couscous was one of the most important dishes to the people of the Middle East and the different ways it was served. When he and Aunt Deborah were through with their story, the crowd rewarded them with a round of vigorous applause and cheers.

Just as the pitch from the party reached its peak, Dad's ears perked up. He and Mom rushed down the stairs and began to bark. Dad, always the consummate watchdog, stood erect and pointed directly at the front door, while Mom jumped and turned in an agitated fashion. Within seconds the doorbell rang.

"My gracious," BJ said, scanning the table. "Who could that be at this time of night, and on Christmas Eve? Everyone, continue eating and talking, and celebrating this wonderful evening. And, thank you, John and Deborah, for a wonderful Christmas story!"

BJ left the table and walked to the front door.

Mom began to pant and bark, and to jump at BJ's skirt. BJ

carefully lifted her into her arms and, continuing to the chime of "I'll Be Home for Christmas" rubbed Mom's head, saying, "I know, darling, it's very hectic with all these people in the house. You can go lay on your cushion whenever you want."

But that was *not* why Mom was excited.

With BJ holding Mom, and with Dad at her side, she opened front door.

What a surprise she saw standing there.

"Merry Christmas," Mr. Bill said. "Did someone in this house lose a puppy?"

The scene that followed is a little blurry in my mind, and Mom's and Dad's, too. But, Sasha later told us that Mom jumped from BJ's arms, and I wiggled free from Mr. Bill's grip. Dad was dumbstruck.

Mom and I rolled into a ball and it could not be seen where she began and I ended. We snuggled and nuzzled and licked each from head to toe. Mom checked for cuts and bruises and bites and kicks. Finally, Dad joined in as well, prancing so fast and furiously that his clicking nails on the tile floor sounded like a herd of reindeer coming through the entryway. This naturally prompted several of the children to spontaneously announce the early arrival of Santa Claus!

BJ, thinking that a wild puffball had been dropped into her house, was helplessly trying to pry Mom and I apart. She sat on the floor with both of us rolling over her lap and through her arms. She was pleading with Dad to help. "Beaux, help Feathers. That little ball is devouring her. Quick, someone, get me a dish of water, we'll have to douse it into submission!"

By now family and friends were running in and out of the

house, the children looking for Santa Claus and his reindeer and the parents looking for their children. It was pandemonium.

Only Mr. Bill and Sasha seemed to be somber and in control.

As if in his classroom, Mr. Bill firmly clapped his hands and announced, "Attention! Attention! Just wait a minute! I think if you take a good look, you'll see that this little puffball belongs to you." This pronouncement almost immediately brought silence to the room. By now all the guests and our whole family had gathered in the entry hall.

In my excitement I had all but forgotten about Sasha and Mr. Bill. Now, hearing his words, I realized that my life was once again about to make a profound change. Mom and I rolled apart and BJ lifted herself up off the floor. Dad stood nose-to-nose with Sasha, and sensing her deep sadness, lifted his paw to her neck and patted it gently. Sasha sunk to the floor, burying her head into the hall carpet.

BJ graciously took the notice from Mr. Bill's hand and after reading it, looked to Mom and me and then over to Dad, and said, "What a wonderful Christmas this has turned out to be." She went to Mr. Bill and hugged him tightly and taking his hand in her's, said, "How can we ever thank you for your kindness? We have all missed our little puppy so much." As her voice trailed off, Mr. Bill bent down to rub my head one last time, and I instinctively jumped into his arms. He rubbed and tickled me before putting me back next to Mom. Then, Mom and I went up to Sasha and the three of us began to rub noses.

Mr. Bill, turning to leave, simply replied, "Merry Christmas." And bid Sasha to come.

As Sasha began to walk down the path with Mr. Bill, Mom,

Dad and I, almost as one dog, began to bark and whine. BJ and all the rest of the family, and guests, too, joined in our protest. "Stop, please. No. No. No. You cannot go without sharing our Christmas celebration!"

Mr. Bill turned and without any command Sasha came bounding back into the beautiful house. Mr. Bill followed. An extra chair was placed at the head of the table, next to BJ, and Sasha took her place on the soft cushions with Mom, Dad, and me. Somehow, looking at Mr. Bill and BJ at the head of the table, I sensed we would be seeing a lot of each other from now on.

The dining room began to settle down, and BJ offered a toast to Mr. Bill and Sasha, entreating him to tell the whole story of my rescue and ultimate return.

Deborah began to place a large scoop of couscous on Mr. Bill's plate, and looking back at BJ she remarked, "Golly, Feathers' little baby is exactly the color of this food. And puffy, too."

Mom and Dad looked up and they, too, recognized there was a similarity.

Seeing their beaming faces, BJ looked at Mr. Bill, and asked what he thought of the name of CousCous for his little former houseguest. Heartily agreeing, it was decided, then and there, that in honor of the holiday and my return to the family, my name would be CousCous.

Uncle Needles, Uncle Willie, and Aunt Bean had been scurrying up and down trees and in and out of bushes to see what all the hubbub was about. As they precariously hung onto a thinning branch of the water oak tree, they could see that Mom and Dad, and I, had been reunited at last. Turning to run down the branches and continue with their holiday celebration, they heard a wise old voice at the base of the oak, saying, "Well, Needles, I guess it will be a Merry Christmas after all."

Needles, looking at his friend, Oldtimer, said, "You're right about that, pal! You're right about that."

A Prayer for Animals

Hear our humble prayer, O God, for our friends the animals. Especially for animals who are suffering, for any that are hunted or lost or deserted or frightened or hungry, for all that must be put to death. We entreat for them all Thy mercy and pity, and for those who deal with them we ask a heart of compassion and gentle hands and kindly words. Make us, ourselves, to be true friends to animals and so share the blessings of the merciful.

—Albert Schweitzer

And from CousCous and her family,
Good Night, dear friends, Good Night.